"Why are you pretending not to know your own wife?"

"Maybe the answer, dear Miss Johnson, is that since my wife was such a spoiled, tiresome woman, I'm doing my best to forget that I was ever married...?"

"Believe me—your wife feels exactly the same way about her crummy, despicable husband!" Flora ground out through clenched teeth.

"That sounds like a fair description of my wife," Ross drawled smoothly. "In fact, it seems as if you've already had the misfortune of meeting the lady. If so, you'll know that she's a bad-tempered, completely self-absorbed person, who's incapable of thinking of anyone or anything—other than her own selfish interests."

"That's a really foul thing to say!" Flora cried. "I'm *not* like that. I..."

"My dear Miss Johnson!" he interjected swiftly. "I was, of course, referring to my wife. Surely you can't imagine that I was talking about *you*?"

MARY LYONS was born in Toronto, Canada, moving to live permanently in England when she was six, although she still proudly maintains her Canadian citizenship. Having married and raised four children, her life nowadays is relatively peaceful—unlike her earlier years when she worked as a radio announcer, reviewed books and, for a time, lived in a turbulent area of the Middle East. She still enjoys a bit of excitement, combining romance with action, humor and suspense in her books whenever possible.

Books by Mary Lyons

HARLEQUIN PRESENTS

MARY LYONS

LYONS

Husband Not Included!

Harlequin Books

TORONTO • NEW YORK • LONDON
AMSTERDAM • PARIS • SYDNEY • HAMBURG
STOCKHOLM • ATHENS • TOKYO • MILAN
MADRID • WARSAW • BUDAPEST • AUCKLAND

ISBN 0-373-11904-6

HUSBAND NOT INCLUDED!

First North American Publication 1997.

PROLOGUE

'IT'S BEEN really great talking to you, Brad. Good luck with your next film—I hear it's going to be a smash hit!'

The auburn-haired reporter gave the young film star a brilliant smile before swirling around to face the TV camera.

'Wow! It's certainly a fantastic party going on here, following the Oscar ceremony,' she continued, her voice almost breathless with excitement. 'I'm hoping to have a word later with some of the really fantastic, mega, *mega* film stars here tonight. But first I'd like you to meet the man who gets my own personal vote for "hunk of the month". Yes, folks, it's the winner of the Oscar for Best Screenplay...*Duncan Ross*!'

The camera swung around to focus on a tall, broad-shouldered figure as the reporter hurried to his side, quickly thrusting a microphone up towards his tanned face.

'Of course, just about *everyone* has read your exciting, action-packed novels. Which is why I'm *so* thrilled to meet you tonight,' she gushed, an eager smile on her lips as she gazed up at the handsome features of the dark-haired man towering over her diminutive figure. 'I'm definitely one of your greatest fans!'

'Er...thank you,' he muttered, clearly uncomfortable at suddenly finding himself in the spotlight.

'I'm told your latest book, *A Time to Live—A Time to*

Die, has been on the New York bestseller list for the past twelve weeks?'

'Yes.'

'And you must be over the moon at having won an Oscar tonight…right?'

He shrugged. 'Yes, I suppose so.'

'But, I bet you never imagined that the film of your book, *Fear No Evil*, would completely sweep the board?'

'No…er…no, I didn't,' he muttered tersely.

'Hey, come on! I've heard all about the famous British reserve, and I can see that you're definitely a modest kinda guy. But, let's try and loosen up here, OK?' the reporter urged, clearly struggling to inject some pizzazz into her interview with such an obviously taciturn and tight-lipped man. 'I mean, it's definitely unusual for a film to win so many Oscars, right?'

He raised a dark, quizzical eyebrow before giving a brief shrug of his broad shoulders. 'I know virtually nothing about the past history of these awards.'

'OK…' She sighed, quickly glancing down at the clipboard in her hand. 'Well, how do you feel about the prize for Best Actress going to the lovely Lois Shelton? I hear that the two of you spent *quite* some time together on location!'

'Oh, really…?' he drawled coldly. 'Maybe you should find better things to do with your time other than listening to idle, foolish gossip.'

'Whoops! I guess that's put *me* in my place!' The reporter gave a shrill peal of hollow laughter as he gazed stonily down at her. 'Well—it's been a *real* pleasure talking to you,' she cooed through gritted teeth, before turning to give the camera a wide smile. 'And now, ladies and gentlemen, let's meet some more of the wonderful, *won-*

derful people here tonight. But first, a word from our sponsor…'

With a deft flick of the remote control, Marty Goldberg switched off the video recording.

'Quite frankly, I've seen better interviews in pitch-dark, under water!' he announced, swivelling around in his chair to face the man sitting on the other side of the desk. 'You're going to have to do a lot better than that in the future, Ross. A *whole* lot better!'

Ross Duncan Whitney gazed silently at his literary agent for a moment, before giving a dismissive shrug of his broad shoulders. 'You know how I loathe all that Hollywood razzmatazz. And I can't stand stupid, empty-headed women. Especially ones asking impertinent questions about my private life,' he added grimly.

'So, who cares about the girl's IQ?' Marty demanded in exasperated tones. 'That reporter was only doing her job. And, besides, she's quite right. You're going to have to learn to loosen up a little and face the fact that you no longer have much of a private life. Because winning the Oscar has made you "News"—whether you like it or not.'

'OK…OK, I've got the message.' Ross sighed, rising to his feet and strolling over to gaze out of the large plate glass window at the skyline of New York city. "So, where do we go from here?'

'Well, your "Duncan Ross" books are continuing to sell like hot cakes. What's more—thanks to the Oscar—we can add another zero to the sum offered by the publishers for your next contract. So, all in all, I'd say that you're now a *very* rich man!'

Ross turned to grin at his agent. 'I'm not likely to complain about that.'

'I should hope not!' Marty laughed. 'And *definitely* not

when you see the terms I've managed to screw out of the film company for the rights on your latest book,' he added, tossing a thick, heavy contract onto the desk in front of him.

'They'll have to find some other writer to do the adaptation, because I'm *never* going to write another screenplay,' Ross announced grimly. 'In fact, rather than have to put up with any more of those neurotic Hollywood filmmakers, I'd prefer to spend the rest of my life working down a Siberian salt mine!'

The older man gave a deep chuckle of laughter. 'OK—I reckon it's now my turn to say that I've got the message. So, what are your plans for the next six months? Will you be returning to that Caribbean island of yours?'

'Yes, I think so. Especially since I want to get the next book to you as soon as possible.'

'OK, that sounds fine. There is just one thing...' The agent paused for a moment, gazing at the tall, dark figure of the man once again clearly buried in thought as he stared out of the window.

Powerfully built, his body all lean muscle and sinew with a mind to match his physical perfection, Ross was certainly nobody's fool. And Marty wasn't looking forward to getting the brush-off from such a very hard, tough man—who was perfectly capable of annihilating a guy with just one scathing glance from those deep blue eyes beneath their heavy lids. There was no way, for instance, that *he* would have made the mistake of asking Ross about his romance with Lois Shelton—a subject which was clearly off-limits as far as his client was concerned.

'I wonder...' Marty cleared his throat. 'I wonder if you'd do me a favour?'

'Sure. What is it?'

'Well, I'm really asking for your help on behalf of my wife. I like to try and keep her happy, and…'

'Oh, Marty!' Ross grinned and shook his dark head. After twenty-five years of marriage, and despite all his friends' dire warnings, the small, tubby agent had insisted on divorcing his wife to marry a blonde bimbo young enough to be his own daughter. 'Is she giving you a hard time?'

'Yeah, you could say that,' the agent muttered, wondering—as he'd done so often lately—whether possessing a 'trophy wife' was all it was cracked up to be. 'But the favour is really for my wife's brother, Bernie Schwartz. He's a real whiz-kid, and earning piles of dough with that cosmetic company he joined a few years ago.'

'So—what's the problem?'

'Well, it isn't exactly a problem, as such. More the fact that Bernie has put together a spectacular advertising campaign which, so my wife tells me, is likely to get him a seat on the board. Unfortunately, with everything all set for "go", there's been some problem with the proposed location.' Marty shrugged. 'To put it in a nutshell, Bernie needs to find a small, virtually uninhabited island in the Caribbean—and as quickly as possible.'

'Hold it!' Ross gave a grim laugh. 'I hope you're not suggesting that he uses Buccaneer Island?'

'Aw…come on, Ross—it wouldn't be for more than a week. And just think about all those sexy young model girls, skipping along the beach with hardly a stitch on. You'd love it!'

'Oh, no, I wouldn't!' Ross growled, turning away from the window to pace up and down the room. 'I was once married to a fashion model, so I know what I'm talking about. Believe me, a more vain, egotistical, selfish bunch of people would be hard to find.'

'Hey—wait until you see the girl who's been chosen to promote the new line of cosmetics.' Marty grinned, ignoring his client's rough words as he spread some large photographs on the desk. 'Bernie says that she's absolutely gorgeous. According to him, she looks just like a Botticelli angel! What do you think?'

Ross gave a heavy sigh as he stopped pacing and strode towards the desk. 'I think both you and your brother-in-law need your heads examined,' he muttered, picking up one of the pictures. 'And why you should imagine I'd want my quiet, peaceful island turned into a damned circus, or have to—' He broke off, his brows drawing together in a sharp frown as he gazed down at the glossy print.

'Nice, huh...?' The older man gave a deep chuckle of laughter. 'I wouldn't mind spending a few days on a desert island with *that* particular girl!'

'What's her name?' Ross demanded curtly, carrying the photograph over to the window to study it more closely.

Marty shrugged. 'I don't know anything about her, except that, like you, she's British—and Bernie clearly thinks she's the best thing since sliced bread!'

There was a long silence as Ross continued to study the picture in his hand. 'You say that your brother-in-law only wants to use my island for a week?' he said at last.

'Yeah—maybe even less,' Marty assured him quickly. 'On top of which, he's more than willing to pay a large fee.'

'Well...if it's only going to be for a few days, I suppose I *could* probably help him out...' Ross drawled slowly.

'Great! And, there's no reason for you to get involved with all the shenanigans if you don't want to. All you have to do is to take off on your yacht, or whatever, and leave them to it.'

'No.' Ross shook his dark head. 'Unfortunately, the small number of staff on the island would never be able to cope on their own. Besides,' he added with a grim bark of sardonic laughter, before abruptly tossing the photograph back down onto the desk, 'I'm beginning to think that this little idea of Bernie's might prove to be very interesting, after all. *Very* interesting indeed!'

CHAPTER ONE

'JUST remember—this is a contract to die for! There are hundreds of gorgeous-looking models who'd give their eye teeth for a chance to be the new Angel Girl. So, whatever happens, *don't* mess up what could be the last chance to resurrect your career.'

Flora Johnson sighed, her lips tightening with apprehension as she recalled the words of her agent, Meredith Taylor, at the end of their celebratory lunch just over a month ago. Turning to stare blindly out of the small window of the aeroplane, she barely noticed the white clouds or the sparkling, azure sky.

Exactly *why* she should be apprehensive about the job which lay ahead of her, she had absolutely no idea. There seemed no sane, sensible reason for her faint, vague feelings of disquiet and unease. She was obviously being ridiculous, and it was time she pulled herself together, she told herself firmly. Anyone who wasn't looking forward, with one hundred percent enthusiasm, to enjoying the warm sandy beaches, blue seas and brilliant sunshine of the Caribbean clearly needed their head examined!

'You've simply got to read this book, Flora. It's absolutely *terrific*!'

'Hmm...?' Flora turned to face the plump, sandy-haired girl sitting in the seat beside her.

Georgie held up the book for her inspection. 'It's the very latest novel by Duncan Ross. Quite honestly, I hardly got a wink of sleep last night!' she added enthusiastically. 'It's *so* exciting that I simply couldn't put it down. I'm on the last chapter, so I'll lend it to you when I'm finished. I know you're going to love it.'

'I doubt it!' Flora muttered, grimacing at the sight of the book's dramatic, vividly coloured dust-jacket—mainly featuring a gruesome, evil-looking dagger dripping with blood. 'To tell you the truth, I really don't care for those sort of "action man" type of books, which I reckon are mostly written for overgrown schoolboys.'

'You're quite wrong—it's not that sort of book at all!' the other girl protested.

Flora merely smiled and shook her head. 'We've got a long flight ahead of us. So I think I'll just try and catch up on some beauty sleep.'

'Come off it!' Georgie gave a hoot of wry laughter, gazing enviously at the thick cloud of tightly curled blonde hair and beautiful features of the slim girl now reclining in the seat beside her. 'As far as I can see, you need more beauty sleep about as much as fish need bicycles!'

'Thanks for the vote of confidence.' Flora grinned before determinedly closing her eyes against any further conversation.

In fact, following the late photographic session last night and an early dash to the airport this morning, she really *was* feeling a bit sleepy. The steady rhythmic background hum of the plane's engines wasn't helping, of course—nor her deep, comfortable seat in the First Class section of the aircraft, which was positively encouraging her to nod off.

And that, now she came to think about it, probably wasn't such a bad idea after all. She knew, from past experience, that the dry, pressurised air in the cabin was likely to play havoc with the texture of her fine, delicate skin. Besides, if she made the mistake of drinking any alcohol during the flight she would undoubtedly find herself arriving at Antigua for their onward flight to a small private island looking thoroughly tired and washed out.

Not that it would normally matter, of course. Most of the passengers on the plane were anticipating a well-earned, relaxing holiday in the sun, well away from the stress and strain of everyday life. So it didn't matter a hoot how weary or crumpled they appeared on their arrival in the Caribbean. Unfortunately, *she* was expected to walk down the steps of the aircraft looking a million dollars—and all ready to grace the pages of high-fashion magazines.

So, while she appreciated Georgie's kind remarks about her looks—which amounted to nothing more than a useful tool, as far as her working life was concerned—Flora knew that the other girl could have no idea of the problems which might lie ahead. Nor of the many difficulties she'd had to face in the past.

Up until just over a year ago, Flora had enjoyed a very successful career as a top fashion and photographic model. Earning huge sums of money, and accustomed to a highly luxurious way of life, she'd foolishly given little thought to such boring, mundane matters as health insurance, or the need to save money for a rainy day.

Which only went to show *just* how much of an idiot she'd been! Because, following that horrendous car accident, which had resulted in a long stay in hospital and an even longer convalescence, she'd not only found herself flat broke—but, with no work in sight, it had also looked as if her career was on the skids as well.

In fact, what she'd have done without her agent, she had no idea. Meredith Taylor, who'd been virtually a mother-figure to Flora ever since she'd run away from home seeking the bright lights of London at the tender age of sixteen, had done her best to calm her fears.

'So, OK—you've been out of the action for some time. But it's not the end of the world,' the older woman had told her firmly. 'Just be patient. Once the word gets around that you're available for work again, I'm sure the jobs will flood in.'

However for Flora, now aged twenty-six and only too well aware of the many fresh, beautiful young girls who were desperately keen to take her place—both on the catwalk and in front of the cameras of world-famous photographers—it had been a nerve-wracking few months. With her phone remaining ominously silent, she had almost given up hope of *ever* working again when she'd received an urgent call from Meredith with the news that a very large American company were desperately looking for a fresh face to launch their new line of cosmetics.

'Get yourself over there as fast as possible,' Meredith had told her urgently, quickly rattling off an address in Mayfair. 'ACE Cosmetics are up against a heavy deadline, so I reckon there's a good chance of you getting the job. But they'll insist on you being as pure as the driven snow,' she'd warned, before explaining that the model who'd originally gained the three-year, multi-million-dollar contract had just been sacked following unfortunate reports in the Press regarding the girl's private life.

'Too many riotous, drug-related late-night parties in Bad Company,' the older woman had added succinctly. 'So, just make sure you come over as squeaky clean. And no mention of your brief marriage to that awful man. Right?'

'Er…right,' Flora had muttered, guiltily suppressing the fact that despite Meredith's strong advice she'd never, somehow, quite got around to arranging a divorce from her husband, whom she hadn't seen for almost six years.

Successfully gaining the job, and almost light-headed with relief at the thought of finally having solved her pressing financial problems, she hadn't taken any particular notice of Meredith's sage advice. But over the past few weeks she'd come to realise that her future prospects might not be quite so rosy after all.

'You might have warned me about that simply *awful* woman!' she'd moaned down the phone to her agent. 'I thought I'd already met most of the fierce, hard-as-nails ladies in this business. But I bet anything you like that Claudia Davidson turns out to be an absolute *nightmare!*'

'What on earth are you talking about? I've never had any problems with Claudia.'

'Well...lucky old you—because she scared me rigid!' Flora retorted grimly. 'I'd hardly entered her glamorous, ultra-modern office to sign the contract when she announced that I was positively the *last* person she'd have chosen for the job. And, she seemed to take great pleasure in pointing out that I was only picked because Mr Schwartz, the American marketing director of ACE Cosmetics, refused to accept any of the other girls she'd got lined up and insisted on me being given the job.'

'Well, if you've got the head honcho rooting for you I can't see that you've got too many problems,' Meredith had responded soothingly.

'Yes, but...'

'Even if you don't particularly like Claudia,' the other woman continued firmly, 'she was amazingly successful at creating a totally new, up-market image for the Elegance Fashion Group. Which is why, I heard, she was headhunted last year by ACE Cosmetics to completely revamp and promote their products for a major assault on the European market. And, in any case,' Meredith added, 'I'm sure you'll find that her bark is far worse than her bite.'

'I should be so lucky!' Flora had ground out glumly, before putting down the phone.

It wasn't just the fact that she and the glamorous, high-powered PR executive in charge of promoting the cosmetic company's new line had taken an instant dislike to one another—although that was likely to mean a difficult working relationship—but Claudia Davidson had also been *very* explicit regarding Flora's new contract.

'I don't want there to be any misunderstandings on your part,' she'd told Flora with an icy smile, her voice carrying a clear warning note of threat and menace.

'As you've seen, your contract stipulates a yearly break clause—with no obligation for the company to explain its reasons for dispensing with your services. On top of which, you must not accept any other work. So, don't let me catch you modelling for any of your old photographer friends—even if you're giving your services for free. Because I'll have you out on your ear so fast, you won't know what's hit you!' she'd added grimly, with what Flora had considered to be quite unnecessary relish.

'The same goes for the fact that we require you to remain single,' the awful woman had continued relentlessly. 'A steady, long-term boyfriend is acceptable, of course. However, since the whole emphasis of the campaign to promote the new Angel Girl will be on her misty, pure and ethereal qualities, we are insisting that your private life must be as clean as a whistle. Do I make myself absolutely clear?'

'Oh, yes—absolutely!' Flora had agreed fervently, her hands shaking slightly as she signed away her life for the next three years.

After all, as she'd consoled herself later, she wasn't likely to have too many problems with most of the clauses in her new contract. Her only regular escort, John Macdonald was a very wealthy and highly respectable merchant banker. And she could see no reason why either Claudia or the cosmetic company should ever find out that she was—in name only, of course—still a married woman.

However, as she now turned to gaze across the aircraft cabin, to where Claudia was sitting beside her principal assistant, Helen Todd, Flora couldn't help feeling slightly apprehensive. Helen, who to all intents and purposes appeared to be a clone of Claudia, and dressed in the same bandbox-fresh, high-fashion resort wear as her senior colleague, wasn't perhaps *quite* so frightening. But there was no doubt that together they made a formidable team.

Only Georgie Wilson, a general dogsbody and 'gofer', who'd been seconded from the cosmetic company to look after Flora, seemed in any way a normal person. It was Georgie, for instance, who'd informed Flora that everyone in the company was terrified of Claudia Davidson.

'She's a *really* scary lady,' Georgie had confided earlier this morning as they'd checked in their baggage at Heathrow Airport, adding with a nervous giggle, 'I'm told that a lot of people in the office refer to her behind her back as "Cruella De Vil"!'

'That sounds a fairly appropriate nickname,' Flora had agreed with a grin, recalling from her childhood the story of *101 Dalmatians* who'd been chased and terrorised by a horrifically frightening woman intent on their slaughter to provide herself with a glamorous fur coat.

However, it was pointless to look for trouble, Flora now told herself firmly. The world of fashion and beauty products contained a considerable number of really awful, highly eccentric and weird people—all given to claiming artistic licence as an excuse for what would normally be thought of as extremely bad behaviour.

So, any model with an ounce of sense normally concentrated on just getting on with the job. And since the company had obtained the services of a world-famous photographer, with whom she'd worked many times in the past, Flora could see no reason why there should be any real problems on this assignment in the Caribbean. Besides, there was definitely no point in crossing any bridges before she came to them. Right?

Busy lecturing herself, Flora found her thoughts sharply interrupted as Georgie gave a loud groan.

'What's wrong?' she asked, quickly sitting up and regarding the other girl with concern. 'Are you feeling all right?

'It's OK—I'm fine,' the other girl told her sadly. 'It's just that I really *hate* finishing a good novel.'

'You are an idiot!' Flora sighed, brushing a tired hand through her long curly hair. She'd already come to the conclusion that maybe the plump, sandy haired girl wasn't too bright. But it now looked as if Georgie was definitely a few sandwiches short of a picnic. 'Why make such a fuss? It's only a book, for heaven's sake!'

'But...but you don't understand. It really was *totally* riveting,' Georgie retorted, ignoring Flora's protests as she firmly placed the large volume on the model's lap. 'There's no harm in at least having a look at the book. I think you'll be surprised.'

'I doubt it!'

'Well, it's been on the New York bestseller list for I don't know how many weeks—so, it's definitely *not* rubbish,' Georgie said firmly as she loosened her seat belt and rose to her feet, before announcing that she was going to stretch her legs.

Still convinced that the book wasn't *at all* her sort of thing, Flora glanced idly down at the blurb inside the front cover. As she had suspected, *A Time to Live—A Time to Die* appeared to be the usual sort of Boys'-Own story concerning espionage and skulduggery in high places.

What sort of guy writes this rubbish...? she asked herself, turning over the book to look at the author's picture on the back cover. She'd never even heard of Duncan Ross, and—*What the hell?*

Suddenly feeling as though she'd been hit very hard in the solar plexus, Flora felt her emerald-green eyes widen with shock as she stared down at the photograph of a dark-haired, ruggedly handsome man. *What on earth was going on?* What was her ex-husband, Ross Whitney, doing with his picture on the back of this book?

How could the publishers have made such a really stupid, *stupid* error? Goodness knows how or why they'd managed to get hold of the wrong photo—but surely the *real* author would be highly indignant at having his identity stolen by a completely unknown mining engineer? A man who was, moreover—certainly as far as she knew—busy working for a large, international company in South America.

Completely stunned, and with her mind in a total whirl, Flora desperately tried to pull herself together. Maybe she was wrong? It had, after all, been almost six years since she'd last seen Ross. And it *was* just a photograph. So, while the author of this book, Duncan Ross, might appear to be the absolute double of her ex-husband, the two men might well turn out to be quite dissimilar in real life. Right?

However, as she stared down at the large black and

white photograph, which took up most of the space on the shiny back cover of the book, Flora could feel the tight knot of apprehension deep in the pit of her stomach gradually swelling into a large, heavy lump of total certainty.

It was no good. There was no point in trying to fool herself. Because, however strange and peculiar it might seem—and however hard she might cling to the hope that it was all a terrible mistake—she had *no* doubt about the identity of the man gazing out at the world with a slightly wry, mocking twist of his lips. She *knew* that it was a photograph of her ex-husband, Ross Whitney. Why, she could even see the faint scar beneath one dark, sardonically raised eyebrow—the result, as she knew only too well, of an accident on the rugby field soon after their wedding.

Besides, there were just too many coincidences for her to swallow. While two men might bear a very strong resemblance to each other, it was *extremely* unlikely that they would also have almost the same name.

Suddenly feeling breathless and dizzy, as if the world was spinning twice as fast as usual on its axis, Flora fell back against her seat, gazing blindly up at the roof of the plane as she tried to sort out the chaotic muddle and confusion in her brain.

Even if it was true, even if she *had* to accept the fact, however weird it might be, that the writer Duncan Ross and her ex-husband Ross Whitney were one and the same person—she could still hardly believe it! Goodness knows, they'd only been married for a very short time. But she had absolutely no recollection of Ross being in any way interested in writing novels. Surely... Well, surely she ought to have seen *some* sign of the fact that he was interested in becoming an author?

She was deeply immersed in trying to solve the conundrum, and her distraught thoughts were interrupted as Georgie returned to her seat.

'Hah! I just *knew* you'd be interested in that book,' Georgie said triumphantly, placing some Duty Free perfume in the overhead locker before lowering her ample curves into the seat beside Flora.

'Well...er...'

'Doesn't he look fantastic? Really drop-dead sexy—if you know what I mean!' Georgie grinned. 'I bet he has girls buzzing around him like bees round a honey-pot.'

Flora, her mind still trying to grapple with the extraordinary fact that her ex-husband appeared to have somehow turned himself into a best-selling author, could only stare blankly at the other girl.

'Well, *you* might not think he's up to much—but as far as I'm concerned he's definitely a bit of all right!' Georgie leaned over to take the book from Flora's lap and gaze down at the photograph of the ruggedly handsome man. 'I just can't *wait* to meet him!'

'Meet him...?' Flora echoed in bewilderment.

So, OK—her brains might be a little scrambled, and she was possibly still reeling from shock, trying to come to terms with the sudden bombshell about her ex-husband's new profession, but even so, Flora knew that the chances of Georgie bumping into a best-selling author—whoever he might be—were just about zero.

'I don't want to dash your hopes,' she told the plump girl, 'but I really don't think there's any likelihood of you meeting the author of this book. Certainly not in the near future.'

'*Of course* I'm going to meet him! After all, he owns Buccaneer Island, doesn't he? Besides,' Georgie added, as if explaining matters to a rather dim child, 'I overheard

Claudia saying that Duncan Ross was definitely going to be on the island, just to make sure that everything ran smoothly. Which is one of the reasons why I've been reading his new book.'

Flora stared at the other girl in shocked silence for some moments. Completely stunned and almost unable to comprehend the appalling, horrific information that in only a few hours' time she was likely to meet again the man she hadn't seen for so many years, it was some moments before she was able to pull herself together.

'Are you seriously telling me that...?'

'Oh, come on!' Georgie grinned. 'Surely you knew that Duncan Ross was the owner of Buccaneer Island?'

Flora shook her dazed head. 'No...no, I had no idea. I mean...I don't understand any of this,' she muttered, feeling as though she'd been suddenly dumped in a foreign country, completely unable either to understand or speak the language.

'I wasn't involved in any of the plans for this trip,' Flora continued, brushing a trembling hand through her long, curly hair. 'I mean...no one's even told me the reason why we're using Buccaneer Island. Surely... Well, surely there must be lots of other places in the Caribbean which are just as suitable for shooting a promotional film. Why didn't they choose Barbados—or Antigua, for heaven's sake?'

'Hey—calm down!' Georgie frowned at the almost hysterical note in the other girl's voice. '*I* didn't make the arrangements. All I know is that Duncan Ross, who owns the island, seems to have some connection with Mr Schwartz, the American marketing director of ACE. And in any case,' she added with a shrug, 'since most countries in the Caribbean have a strict law about their beaches always being open to members of the public, maybe it's a good idea not to have too many people cluttering up the scene? Especially if you're likely to be prancing half-naked over the sand.'

'I never prance—and certainly not half-naked!' Flora snapped, before quickly realising that it was totally unfair to take her shock and frustration out on Georgie. 'I'm sorry,' she muttered, with a brief, apologetic smile. 'It looks as though I must have got out of the wrong side of the bed this morning.'

'That's OK—forget it.' Georgie gave her a friendly grin, clearly used to dealing with the more temperamental, prima donna type of model. 'I'm really looking forward to the next few days. I haven't been to the Caribbean before, and I can't wait...'

Leaning back, allowing her mind to drift as the other girl continued to expand on the delights awaiting them all on Buccaneer Island, it was some moments before Flora suddenly realised that her troubles were now multiplying with the speed of light.

Oh, Lord—she'd forgotten all about her contract!

Claudia Davidson had been brutally frank about the cosmetic company's basic rules: not only was Flora required to be pure in thought and deed—but they were also insisting on her being *single*! And yet within a few hours it was almost certain that she would be meeting the man who she regarded as her *ex*-husband...but to whom she was—alas!—still *married*.

Feeling totally sick to the pit of her stomach, she could see no way of avoiding the swift, ruthless and hideously embarrassing termination of her contract. And that wasn't all. Not by a long chalk! She could virtually guarantee the fact that Claudia would go completely *ballistic* on discovering the truth about Flora's marital status. And ACE weren't exactly going to be whistling for joy either.

Shivering with fright, and trying to control her trembling limbs, Flora realised that she was now in deep, *deep* trouble. She had no doubt that the company would be in a strong position if they decided to take her to court in order to recover the costs involved in setting up this trip to the Caribbean. Because even if she hadn't told an outright lie she'd still put her signature to a contract containing a clause which she had known to be false.

How *could* she have been such a fool? There was no way she would ever be able to repay the company's expenses. In fact, if she'd been worried about her financial position before being offered this job it was a mere bagatelle when compared to the total bankruptcy which she was likely to face in the future.

Seething with frustration and anger, both at the malign fate which was about to engulf her and the incredibly foolish, outright stupidity of not having divorced Ross years ago, Flora struggled to contain her mounting hysteria, quite certain that her head was going to explode with pent-up rage and fury. But, as she continued to fulminate and rail against her own folly, she realised that there was absolutely nothing she could do to prevent the inevitable, total disaster which lay ahead.

Some hours later, as the small private plane which had been hired to transport them from Antigua slowly circled over the landing site on Buccaneer Island, Flora still hadn't been able to find a solution to her problem. Certain that she'd never felt quite so frightened in all her life, she was in such a state of mental exhaustion that she couldn't think of *anything* except the truly horrendous fate which awaited her just as soon as they landed.

It was almost as if she'd suddenly developed St Vitus's Dance, she thought, miserably aware that her knees were knocking together like castanets. But, as the plane descended rapidly towards the green, grassy strip which lay alongside a wide sandy beach, she made a supreme effort to try and pull herself together.

Carefully descending the steps of the aircraft on legs which felt as though they were made of jelly, Flora found herself trailing behind Claudia Davidson and her entourage, who were walking briskly towards a small group of people clearly awaiting their arrival. Through the haze of shimmering heat, her eyes were slowly and forcibly drawn towards a man standing slightly apart from the others, leaning nonchalantly against a rather battered-looking old Land Rover.

Feeling suddenly faint, she was almost physically aware of the blood draining from her face at the sight of the tall, broad-shouldered figure and tanned, arrogant features of the person she hadn't seen for so long. Drawing on her positively last reserves of courage, she took a deep, shuddering breath.

Here goes nothing! Flora told herself defiantly, putting on the performance of a lifetime as she walked slowly and steadily, with her head held high, towards her ex-husband, Ross Whitney. The man who, within the next few minutes, was almost certainly going to blow her world sky-high.

CHAPTER TWO

DELIBERATELY forcing herself to appear outwardly calm and collected, Flora knew her mind was in a complete turmoil as she walked slowly towards the husband she hadn't seen for so many years.

Amongst all her other overwhelming problems, she now realised that she'd completely forgotten to put on her dark glasses. Not only would they have offered protection from the harsh rays of the sun, but—ridiculous as it might seem—she'd have felt a whole lot safer with her eyes well hidden behind the black shades. Unfortunately there was no way she could now begin fumbling through her large handbag. Not when she was striving with all her might to appear so cool and laid-back.

Despite knowing that total disaster lay only a few moments away, she couldn't seem to stop her brain from frantically buzzing with completely hopeless, totally impractical plans of escape. But even as she desperately thought of trying to reach Ross before the others—and somehow managing to persuade him to keep quiet about their marriage—she knew that it was now far, *far* too late for any hope of rescue.

'Ah, Mr Ross...!' Claudia called out imperiously, ignoring the small group of people standing by an open truck as she strode purposefully towards the tall figure leaning nonchalantly against his vehicle.

'We're *so* grateful to you for allowing us to use this

lovely island of yours,' she told him with a beaming smile as she introduced herself and her faithful shadow, Helen Todd. 'I understand that you're a friend of that clever young businessman, Mr Schwartz?'

'Well, no—not exactly,' the tall man drawled. 'Although I know his brother-in-law very well, I haven't yet had the pleasure of meeting Bernie. However, I understand he is due to join us later on today,' he added, before explaining that he only used the pseudonym 'Duncan Ross' for his books. 'So, please call me Ross—and I hope you enjoy your stay on Buccaneer Island.'

'I'm quite sure we will!' Claudia trilled, smiling coyly up at the handsome man, a faint flush on her cheekbones as she nervously patted her hair.

Slowly coming to a halt beside them, Flora had been momentarily distracted from her own fear and trepidation by the amazing sight of that normally hard, tough and ruthless woman Claudia Davidson now simpering like a bashful schoolgirl. But she found herself being suddenly jerked back to harsh, cruel reality as Ross turned slowly to face her.

'Oh yes...' Claudia waved a limp, heavily ringed hand in Flora's direction. 'This is Miss Flora Johnson. She's going to be the model for our Angel Girl campaign.'

'An "angel girl"...? Well, well!' Ross drawled, his vivid blue eyes beneath their heavy lids glinting with sardonic amusement as he gazed down at Flora. And then, with what she could only think of as bare-faced insolence, he proceeded to conduct an analytical appraisal of her, beginning at the top of her curly head and travelling slowly down over her slim figure before coming to a halt at the pink toenails of her feet in their light sandals.

Damned cheek! Flora gritted her teeth, fuming with resentment and anger. Despite feeling quite faint and sick with dread of the forthcoming explosion, which she knew could be only seconds away, she was sorely tempted to give his face a good, hard slap. How *dared* the foul man treat her as if she were standing there stark naked?

'However, you won't be seeing very much of her,' Claudia continued in a dismissive tone of voice. 'When she isn't in front of the camera, Miss Johnson will have to stay indoors during the heat of the day, to make sure that she doesn't get too suntanned.'

'Really...?' Ross murmured, lifting a dark, sardonic eyebrow as he blandly regarded the flushed cheeks and angry glint in the large green eyes of the girl standing beside him. 'That doesn't sound much fun.'

'Miss Johnson is not here to have "fun",' the older woman corrected him sharply, clearly annoyed that he was paying attention to anyone other than herself. 'This is strictly a working assignment as far as she is concerned. Isn't that right, *dear*?' she added, turning her hard, beady eyes in Flora's direction.

Numb with fear of the storm about to break over her head any moment—and quailing beneath the grim note of warning in Claudia's voice—Flora could only give a weak nod of agreement.

'Never mind, Miss...er...Johnson,' Ross drawled coolly. 'I'll certainly do my best to make sure that your "working assignment" proves to be a pleasant and... er...an interesting one.'

The other two women might have missed it, but Flora had no difficulty in hearing the low, ironic note of grim amusement which lay beneath Ross's bland words. He's playing with me, she thought, staring down at the ground for a moment before slowly raising her head to find herself being regarded by blank blue eyes and a cool smile which held no hint of recognition.

Totally confused, for a few brief seconds she almost managed to convince herself that Ross really *didn't* know who she was. But then, as he gave her a swift, piercing glance before turning back to the two older women, she realised that she'd been momentarily living in a fool's paradise. Whatever game he might be playing, it certainly wasn't good news for her—not if that harsh gleam in his eyes and the cruel, mocking curve of his lips was anything to go by.

Unfortunately, she was given no time in which to mull over the question of exactly why Ross appeared to be pretending not to know her. Almost before she knew what was happening, she was being swept up in the general melee as they were joined by Georgie, and the small group of people who'd come to meet the plane.

With her mind in a complete daze, Flora barely noticed the luggage being loaded onto a truck which soon vanished into the distance. Nor was she given any time to acknowledge the loud, cheerful greetings from some of her old acquaintances. In what seemed the twinkling of an eye, she found herself seated beside Georgie in the back of Ross's large open Land Rover, with Helen and various pieces of hand luggage occupying the bench seat in front of them, and being driven along a grass track edging a wide, sandy beach.

Luckily there was no need for her to say or do anything, since Claudia, seated in the front passenger seat next to Ross, was clearly intent on claiming his full attention.

Finally managing to find and put on her dark glasses, Flora knew that if she hadn't been feeling so sick with nerves she'd have been able to appreciate the amusing, grim irony of being grateful to the awful woman. Thanks to Claudia's determination to monopolise Ross's attention she was being given a short break in which to try and get her act together. But, gazing blindly out of the vehicle, she was unable to savour the entrancing view of pale white sand and sparkling blue sea. Not when her whole attention was now focused on the one, overriding problem: how to prevent her ex-husband from spilling the beans?

She had no idea why Ross was pretending not to know her. He appeared to have transformed himself into a very successful author and had clearly made a new life for himself here, in the Caribbean. So, maybe he regretted their brief marriage as much as she did? However, as long as he didn't open his mouth and 'tell all' before she had a chance to get him on his own and swear him to secrecy about their brief marriage, it was *just* possible that she might be able to prevent her career from going down the tubes.

Preoccupied with her overwhelming problems, it was some time before Flora noticed that they had left the coastline of the small island behind them and were now speeding inland along a grass track bordered on each side by shady groves of palm trees. On reaching a clearing, she saw that they faced a large plantation house whose green lawns were surrounded by brightly coloured trees and shrubs. But, instead of driving up to the house, their vehicle veered off to the side, winding its way through yet more palms and banana trees heavy with fruit before coming to a halt outside a small wooden building.

As Ross jumped out, helping Claudia and Helen down from the vehicle before leading them towards the front door, where their suitcases awaited them, Flora studied the tiny cottage. It looked enchanting, with a bright red corrugated metal roof set over white walls, a pale pink front door and window frames, and the whole surrounded by a pretty pink and white wooden veranda. She was just thinking that it must be every little girl's dream—a large, magnificent dolls' house of their very own—when Georgie gave her a sharp dig in the ribs.

'How about this for a taste of luxury! Not bad, huh?'

'Hmm…?'

'Come on, Flora! Have you been asleep or what?' Georgie stared at her in surprise. 'Didn't you hear Ross say that we're all being allocated separate guest cottages?'

'No, I…''

'He was telling Claudia that this type of local building is known as a popular house, or "case",' Georgie explained quickly as Ross helped the older women with their luggage. 'Apparently, they were originally designed for families who worked on the old sugar plantations, and are still used throughout the Caribbean. So, Ross decided they'd make perfect guest suites for his visitors and had some prefabricated units shipped over from Antigua,' she added, peering through the trees towards where other small pastel-coloured buildings were scattered haphazardly amongst the lush vegetation. 'I can't wait to see mine.'

However, after Ross had dropped Georgie off at her cottage—which she was apparently sharing with the make-up and hair stylist—the atmosphere within the vehicle became positively glacial. Fully determined to sort matters out as quickly as possible, Flora was thrown completely off-base at being roughly ordered by her ex-husband to sit in the front passenger seat.

'I don't mind driving everyone to their cottages. But I'm damned if I'm going to act as a hired chauffeur to some flibbertigibbet model!' he growled, waiting with barely concealed impatience as she hurriedly changed seats.

'OK…OK, there's no need to be so rude,' she snapped,

furious with herself for having so instinctively obeyed his harshly voiced command. '*I* didn't make the arrangements to stay on this island. So how am I expected to know how you run things? In fact,' she added grimly, 'I'd never have come within a mile of the damned place—not if I'd known *you'd* be here!'

He gave a low bark of sardonic laughter, which only served to inflame her already raw nerves to screaming pitch.

'Now, now, Miss Johnson,' he murmured, 'there's no need to lose your temper.'

'Oh, no…?' she ground out through gritted teeth. 'Well, that's all you know! Because it looks as if losing my temper is the very *least* of my problems. And what's with this "Miss Johnson" nonsense anyway?' she added belligerently, turning to scowl at his handsome tanned profile. 'You know very well who I am.'

'Of course I know who you are,' he drawled coolly as he brought the Land Rover to a halt outside a cottage screened from the other small houses by a thick hedge of flowering shrubs. 'I've just been told that you're Bernie Schwartz's new Angel Girl. I also have it on good authority—from his own brother-in-law, no less—that Bernie seems to think you're the best thing since sliced bread. How about that?'

'Oh, for heaven's sake!' she exploded as he switched off the ignition. 'Why on earth are you playing these stupid games?'

'"Games", Miss Johnson?' He raised a dark, satanic eyebrow as he gazed at her with a bland, cool smile on his lips. 'I've no idea what you're talking about.'

'Oh, yes, you damn well do!' she accused him bleakly, grimly aware of the dark, insidious attraction of the man lounging so casually in his seat beside her. Maybe if she hadn't been feeling quite so tired and exhausted, she would have been better equipped to ignore the muscular shoulders beneath the thin fabric of his short-sleeved cream shirt, and the long-fingered, strong hands lightly grasping the wheel.

Life was so unfair! Surely, if there was any justice in the world, Ross ought to have gone thoroughly to seed over the past six years? Unfortunately—instead of having become seriously overweight, with a paunch and receding hairline—he was still fit, slim, lithe and as diabolically attractive as ever. Besides which, there ought to be a law against allowing men to wear shorts, she told herself acidly. Because the sight of Ross's bare, deeply tanned and muscular brown legs almost touching her own was definitely *not* helping her to concentrate on her problems.

Making a supreme effort to pull herself together, Flora took a deep breath.

'Leaving aside the other interesting questions, such as how a one-time mining engineer has managed to become a best-selling author,' she told him scathingly, 'what I *really* want to know is why he's also pretending not to know his wife?'

'You're right—that's definitely an interesting question,' he drawled mockingly as he got out and came around to her side. 'Maybe the answer, dear Miss Johnson, is that since my wife was such a spoilt and tiresome woman I'm doing my best to forget that I was ever married...'

'Believe me—your wife feels *exactly* the same way about her crummy, despicable husband!' she ground out through clenched teeth, swearing under her breath as she tried to open the passenger door. 'I *really* hate these trendy four-wheel-drive vehicles!' she muttered, savagely banging her fist on the dashboard. Only to find herself becoming even more furious as he gave an infuriating chuckle of laughter.

'Oh, dear—we really *do* seem to be losing our temper, don't we?' he murmured, calmly opening the door before scooping up her in-flight bag from the rear seat and walking towards the small blue and white cottage.

'You...you damned man!' she shouted furiously, tumbling out of the Land Rover and almost running to keep up with him as he strode up the steps to the front door. 'You always were bloody-minded, and...and as obstinate as a pig!'

Calmly placing a key in the lock, he opened the door before turning slowly towards her. 'That sounds a fair description of my wife,' he drawled smoothly. 'In fact, it seems as if you've already had the misfortune of meeting the lady. If so, you'll know that she's a bad-tempered, completely self-absorbed person, who's quite incapable of thinking of anyone or anything—other than her own selfish interests.'

'That's a really foul thing to say!' she cried. 'I'm *not* like that. I—'

'My dear Miss Johnson!' he interjected swiftly. 'I was, of course, referring to my wife. Surely you can't imagine that I was talking about *you*? Especially since you're apparently such a very, *very* good friend of Bernie Schwartz,' he added, the bland smile on his lips sharply at variance with the bleak, chilly gleam in his blue eyes.

Flora stiffened. 'And just what's that last snide remark supposed to mean?'

Ignoring her tense, angry figure, Ross merely shrugged his broad shoulders before carrying her luggage into the main sitting room of the cottage.

Trailing slowly behind him, Flora realised that she'd been acting like an utter fool. She might loathe this hateful man, but trading insults wasn't going to achieve anything. Not when she needed his assistance to save her career. Unfortunately, however much it might stick in her throat, she had no alternative but to eat Humble Pie.

'Look...I'm sorry if I lost my temper just now,' she told him stiffly. 'It's been a long day, and I expect I'm suffering from jet lag. But the thing is...I've got a problem and I need your help.'

'*My* help...?' He gave a scornful laugh. 'You must be joking! If you want to cry on someone's shoulder I suggest that you'd better go and weep all over Bernie Schwartz.'

'Oh—for heaven's sake!' Flora gave an impatient, heavy sigh. 'That's the whole problem. I *can't* discuss this matter with Mr Schwartz.'

Ross studied her grimly for a moment. 'Do I gather that congratulations are in order?'

'What...?' she muttered, frowning at him in confusion.

'You and Bernie, of course.'

'Well, I'm obviously pleased to have got this job, if that's what you mean. But the fact is that Mr Schwartz, and everyone at ACE Cosmetics—not to mention that awful Claudia woman—all think that I'm single. It's in the contract, you see.'

He shrugged. 'No—I'm afraid that I don't see,' he retorted, before turning to leave the room.

'Oh, *please*...!' she cried, swiftly grabbing hold of his arm and hurriedly explaining the situation in which she now found herself. 'And if they find out I'm still married to you I'll be for the high jump,' she added desperately. 'You've simply *got* to help me.'

Ross stared at her silently for what seemed a long, long time.

'Well, well...the plot thickens, doesn't it?' he said

slowly, studying her intently from beneath his heavy lids.
'So, you want me to pretend that we've never met before
now?'

'Why not? After all, you were giving a very good im-
pression of not knowing who I was when we landed from
the aircraft just now,' she pointed out quickly. 'The point
is: it's *vitally* important that everyone connected with
ACE continues to believe that I've never been married.'

'But why should I help you?' Ross drawled coolly. 'It's
no skin off my nose if you get sacked from this job.'

'How *can* you do this to me?' she moaned, waving her
hands distractedly in the air.

He laughed. 'Very easily! In fact, it might be quite
amusing to stand by and watch the balloon go up.'

'Oh, that's *great*—thanks a bunch!' she stormed.
'Leopards never change their spots. So, I should have realised that you're still the same thoroughly obnoxious, rotten bastard who walked out on me all those years ago.
Right?'

As she saw his lips tightening into a grim, narrow line,
and the dark flush of colour beneath his tanned cheeks,
she was gripped by a sharp sense of fierce satisfaction.
Despite knowing that she was every bit as much to blame
for the break-up of their marriage, Flora was finding enormous release in being able—at long last!—to give voice
to her deeply buried feelings of painful heartache and bitter, dark resentment at the way she'd been treated.

'I'm amazed that our marriage lasted as long as it did.'
She gave a shrill, high-pitched laugh. 'It was just like you
to waltz off and leave me without even one word of explanation!'

'As I recall, there were plenty of "words",' he ground
out in a clipped, hard voice as he took a determined step
towards her. 'But would you listen to anything I had to

say? Oh, no—that was asking too much, wasn't it?' he added grimly, catching hold of her arm as she tried to turn away. 'You were *far* too preoccupied with your so-called glamorous career—too full of yourself and too damn selfish to pay any attention to your husband.'

'And what right did you have to expect me to throw up everything I'd worked for just because you'd been offered a job in some fly-blown, disease-ridden jungle in South America?' she snarled, desperately trying to wriggle out from beneath his powerful grip on her shoulders. 'Did you listen to anything *I* had to say? Did you hell!'

'That was different,' he growled.

'Oh, right! So you admit that there was one law for you as my husband—and quite another for me in the role of wife...? Nice one, Ross!' she grated scornfully. 'Besides, I notice that *you* clearly didn't stay in South America for more than five minutes. So, it looks as if I made the right decision after all!'

'You always were a first-class bitch!' he hissed, pulling her struggling figure hard up against the length of his tall, firm body.

'And you were always a total *bastard*!' she panted. 'If I'm going down the tubes with ACE I'll damn well take you with me. I'll tell them—I'll tell the whole wide world just what a vile, rotten...devious...'

But even as Flora hunted frantically in her mind for a few more nasty adjectives to describe her foul husband she was forcibly silenced as he swiftly lowered his dark head. A brief second later his lips were on hers, fierce and contemptuous, as though he intended to totally drain her of the will to defy him ever again.

Her heartbeat was pounding like a sledgehammer beneath the stormy force of his cruel mouth, her soft breasts crushed tightly against his hard frame, and she knew that

Ross was using this kiss as a punishment for her defiance; the brutal arrogance of his flesh was demanding her complete submission to his iron will.

Not until she was almost fainting, her tired and weary body trembling weakly against him, did she feel his lips softening for a few, brief moments before he slowly raised his dark head.

There was a long silence, broken only by the sound of their heavy breathing, and she stared numbly up at Ross, too emotionally exhausted to say or do anything, knowing that without the support of his arms she would have slumped helplessly to the floor.

But if she was incapable of speech he seemed to have no problem in finding his voice.

'I've no intention of apologizing for what happened just now,' he grated. 'And if you've got any sense in that beautiful head of yours—which I very much doubt— you'll keep well out of my way for the rest of your stay on this island.'

'Don't...don't you dare threaten me, you...you foul bully!' she gasped huskily. 'Believe me, if I had one of my father's shotguns to hand I wouldn't think twice before putting a bullet through *your* stupid head!'

'You're all heart, darling,' he murmured sardonically. 'But then, I always say that you can take the girl out of the farmyard—but you can't take the farmyard out of the girl. And it looks as if I'm right—especially if your new "rustic" hairstyle is anything to go by,' he added scornfully, lifting a curly lock of her long blonde hair.

'Leave me alone!' she snapped, unable to prevent an involuntary shiver at the touch of his fingers brushing against her skin.

He gave a short bark of angry laughter as he spun on his heel and marched swiftly towards the door. 'Don't worry—I've got far better ways of spending my time than dancing attendance on an empty-headed blonde bimbo!'

'Get lost!' she yelled, almost beside herself with rage. 'And I hope I live long enough to dance on your grave!'

'I'm sure that you will, Flora,' he drawled coolly.

Opening the door, he paused in the doorway, his tall, broad-shouldered figure a dark silhouette against the bright sunlight as he delivered his parting shot. 'But at least I'll have the satisfaction—when I'm six feet under and pushing up the daisies—of not having to watch the last waltz being performed by a wizened, lonely, toothless old hag!'

Shaking with nervous exhaustion, her ears ringing with the loud bang of the front door being slammed shut behind Ross's departing figure, Flora waited with bated breath until she heard the sound of his vehicle fading away in the distance. Only then did she feel capable of staggering a few feet across the floor, before sinking down into a rattan chair.

Trust the bastard Ross Whitney to make sure that he had the last word! she told herself grimly, shutting her eyes for a moment and allowing the waves of mental and physical exhaustion to flood through her weary body.

Goodness knows, almost from the first moment that she'd succeeded in gaining the Angel Girl contract she had been troubled by bad vibes about the job. And how right she'd been! Because this whole trip to the Caribbean had been clearly doomed from the start. And now, having stupidly thrown away her only opportunity of gaining the support of Ross, there seemed no way of avoiding the forthcoming disaster.

How could she have been such a blithering idiot? It wasn't as though she was a teenager and didn't know any better. She was supposed to be a sophisticated woman of twenty-six, for heaven's sake! So, why on earth had she allowed herself to become involved in a stupid, no-holds-barred fight with Ross? And to have effectively torpedoed her only chance of solving her problems with the cosmetic company?

Groaning out loud at her own folly, Flora buried her face in her hands for a moment. Unfortunately, it was no good putting all the blame for the disastrous scene which had just taken place on Ross. Although it had been partly his fault, of course. The foul, rotten man had always known how to make her madder than a hornets' nest—in just about five seconds flat—but there'd been absolutely *no* call for some of those nasty, snide remarks.

All the same…maybe if her nerves hadn't been at screaming point, after such a long and tiring day, she might have been able to cope with her ex-husband. He had, after all, been the one who'd deserted her—suddenly vanishing into thin air, never to be seen again from that day to this—leaving her to face the lonely tears and all the problems involved in sorting out the shattered pieces of their brief marriage.

In fact, now she came to think about it, Ross had obviously been having the time of his life here in the Caribbean. While she'd been slaving away on the catwalk and in front of the cameras, her swine of a husband had probably been living the life of Reilly: swigging rum, making love to dusky maidens and writing those rubbishy books of his.

Nice work if you can get it! she told herself grimly. So, what now gave him the right to claim the moral high ground? Why was he still bothering to blame *her* for what had happened in the past?

However, despite running the disastrous scene back and forth through her tired mind, she failed to find any answers to those questions. In fact, she only succeeded in giving herself a thumping headache.

Realising that she couldn't sit in the chair all day, Flora wearily began to unpack her cases. After taking some aspirins, and deciding that maybe a shower and a change of clothes might at least make her feel slightly better, she made her way to the small bathroom.

Unfortunately, even after showering and washing her hair, she still felt nerve-rackingly tense and jittery. Which wasn't surprising, she told herself glumly. That encounter with Ross had been bad enough, but it was nothing to the explosion which was likely to break over her head once Claudia learned that she was married. And to have even hoped that her lousy ex-husband would help to save her bacon had been foolish in the extreme.

Gazing dispiritedly at herself in the dressing table mirror, trying to ignore the strained expression on her pale face as she dragged a brush through her damp curls, she cursed her ex-husband's good memory. It had clearly been a bad, bad mistake to have ever told Ross about her past. Because he obviously hadn't been able to resist the cruel jibe he'd made about her upbringing on the farm in Cumberland. And, knowing the swine, he'd undoubtedly have a lot of fun telling everyone on the island about it as well.

She gave a heavy sigh. There was nothing she could do if Ross decided to broadcast the news. But so what if he did? She was over twenty-one years of age. And besides, she was sufficiently successful nowadays not to care if her father, or her dreaded stepmother, did try to track her down, Flora told herself defiantly, gazing blindly into the mirror as she recalled the harsh memories of her childhood.

The only child of elderly parents, she had grown up on a large farm in the north of England. An ugly, gawky little

girl—originally christened Florence, but more generally
known as 'our Flo'—she'd been fiercely protective of her
weak, fragile mother, who'd died when her daughter was
only fourteen.

Not that her father was a cruel man, Flora quickly reminded herself. It was just that such a dour and stern,
upright churchgoing man had clearly had no time or in-
clination to cope with a teenage daughter—not when he
would obviously have preferred to have fathered a son,
who could have been of some use on the farm. However,
if Flora had hoped that following her mother's death both
she and her father could have forged a new and warmer
relationship, she had been doomed to disappointment.
Only a few months after her mother's death, Mr Johnson
had announced that he was marrying a widow who owned
a large farm adjacent to his own.

Unfortunately, her father's announcement that his new
wife and 'our Flo' were bound to get on like a house on
fire, proved to be entirely false. Flora and her stepmother
had hated each other on sight. And since the new Mrs
Johnson had brought to her marriage not only a large farm
but also two large, aggressive sons from her first marriage,
Flora had found herself virtually frozen out of the new
family, being treated as an unwelcome guest in what had
once been her own home.

With hindsight, Flora could now see that her stepmother hadn't been entirely to blame for the two years of
misery that followed. Having to cope with a rebellious
teenager was clearly enough to try the patience of a saint.
And the difficult situation had been further exacerbated
by the fact that as Flora had turned fifteen the once plain,
awkward child had rapidly developed into an outstandingly beautiful girl, attracting the unwelcome attention of
her two stepbrothers.

Flora had loathed what she thought of as the great, glumping, hairy boys, and spent as much time as she could in the homes of her schoolfriends, accompanying them on holiday whenever possible. Which was why, in a moment of teenage bravado, she and her best friend, Vicky, had entered a modelling competition when on holiday with Vicky's parents in Bournemouth, on the south coast.

Flora could shudder now as she looked back at her young, teenage self, prancing around the stage in fits of giggles with absolutely no idea of how to even walk in a straight line. And she hadn't won, of course. It had, after all, been nothing more than a lark. Which was why she'd been astounded to be approached after the competition by a scout from the Meredith Taylor Agency, whose clients apparently included many of the top international names in the modelling business.

Arriving home and informing her father and stepmother that she was being entered by the agency for the "Look of the Year" competition, she had been at first downcast and then rebelliously angry at being told there was no way they would allow her to partake. However, having by then turned sixteen, and with the bit firmly between her teeth, Flora had been determined to grab an opportunity—*any* opportunity—of escaping from what had become a very unhappy home life. And so, waiting until the coast was clear, she'd managed to hitch a lift into the nearest big town, where she'd caught a fast train to London.

What an idiot I was! Flora told herself now, almost shuddering at the thought of how, like so many silly young girls, she could have ended up amongst the flotsam and jetsam, sleeping rough on the streets of the capital city. However, with the Meredith Taylor Agency looking after her, Flora had easily won the competition, and within months she was appearing on the catwalks of Paris and Milan.

She had invented a new personality for herself by officially changing her name to Flora Johnson and claiming to have been born somewhere north of the border in Scotland—and over the next few years her career had taken off like a rocket. Not afraid of hard work—especially as it was nothing to the tough, physical labour used on the family farm—and ruthlessly ambitious to achieve both the stardom and the high-earning power of the top models, Flora had remained totally committed to her career. Which was why, even now, she completely failed to understand why she'd allowed herself to be persuaded to visit that low dive of a nightclub in Paris.

It was such an incredibly stupid thing to have done. And not only because she'd needed an early night before a busy photographic session the next morning. If she *had* remained in her hotel bedroom, she'd never have made the really bad mistake of meeting that awful man—Ross Whitney!

Giving herself a quick shake, Flora firmly suppressed the hurtful memories of her brief marriage. There was no point in trawling over that ground again. And if she *was* going to have to face the music this evening, it might be a good idea to put her feet up for a few minutes.

Fully intending only to have a short nap, she was woken by the strident ringing of a telephone, and was horrified to discover that it was now pitch-dark. Fumbling for a switch on the bedside table, it then took her some time to locate the phone, eventually tracking it down to a small table in the adjacent sitting room.

'Flora! What in the hell are you doing?'' Ross's voice grated harshly in her ear.

'I...I must have fallen asleep,' she muttered. 'What time is it?'

'It's time to get your act together and get yourself over here, to my house,' he retorted curtly. 'I'm holding a welcome party for ACE.'

'No...er...I think I'll just go back to bed,' she told him with a heavy yawn. 'I can't think of anything worse than having to make jolly conversation with Claudia and the other members of ACE. Besides which, drinks parties aren't really my thing. So, if you'd make my excuses, and—'

'Forget it! Your boyfriend, Bernie, has just flown in, and is impatiently waiting to see his "Botticelli angel".' Ross's voice was harsh and scathing. 'So, if you don't want me to tell everyone about our little secret...I'll expect to see you in five minutes.'

'That...that's blackmail!' she wailed helplessly.

He gave a short bark of cruel laughter. 'You're so right, darling,' he taunted, before the line went dead.

I'll kill him! Flora told herself viciously, before realising that she couldn't afford to spend any time plotting vengeance on her ex-husband. Not when the rat had given her only a few precious minutes in which to try and save her career.

CHAPTER THREE

FLORA had no illusions about the so-called 'welcome party'. In fact, she was quite certain that the chances of it being anything other than agonisingly stressful and fraught with tension were just about zero.

However, years of practice on the catwalks—which always involved frantic, swift changes of clothing behind the scenes—now stood her in good stead. Only three minutes after the phone call from Ross she was standing breathless but fully dressed in a pale green little chiffon number, which skimmed lightly down over her tall, slim figure. Quickly slipping on some high-heeled gold sandals, and checking that her make-up didn't look too awful—there was virtually nothing she could do to tame her cloud of newly washed, long curly hair—she ran towards the front door.

It was only when she emerged out onto the veranda of her guest cottage that Flora realised she had a major problem. How the heck was she going to find her way to Ross's house? Peering through the darkness of the warm Caribbean night, she could see faint lights twinkling in the distance. Unfortunately she'd been feeling so uptight on the journey from the airport—and then so busy quarrelling with her ex-husband—that she hadn't taken any particular notice of the winding, twisting route over which Ross had driven to her cottage.

Biting her lip with indecision, Flora wished she didn't

feel so nervous about launching herself off into the darkness. She wasn't too worried about the high-pitched chirping of crickets in the long grass, however, it was definitely unnerving to hear a nearby, ominously low, croaking noise from what sounded like *huge* fat green frogs.

She knew it was pathetic—not to say feeble-minded— to be afraid of such harmless creatures. But, as far as she was concerned, just the mere thought of frogs, toads and snakes was enough to make her break out in a cold sweat.

Trying to pluck up enough courage to leave the safety of the veranda, she was startled to find herself suddenly blinded by the harsh blaze of large spotlights.

'Very good, Flora! I make that just four and a half minutes, precisely.'

Oh, no! She'd know that voice anywhere.

'What…what's going on?' she protested, raising an arm to shield her eyes from the dazzling glare of what she could now see were the headlights of a vehicle.

'Hurry up!' Ross called out tersely. 'I can't sit around here all night. I've got to get back to my guests.'

'I thought I'd told you to get lost,' Flora grumbled as she climbed into the passenger seat beside him.

Ross gave a harsh laugh as he switched on the ignition and slammed the Land Rover into gear. 'So you did. But I seem to recall—although I can't for the life of me think why—that you used to be frightened of creepy-crawlies. Not to mention slimy snakes and—'

'OK…OK—I've got the message,' she muttered hurriedly. Nervously clutching her seat as he put his foot hard down on the accelerator, she added with bad grace, 'I…well, I suppose I ought to say thank you for coming to get me.'

'It might not be a bad idea,' he agreed coldly. 'However, I'm really doing this for your boyfriend. He was so clearly disappointed at your absence, I hadn't the heart to ruin his evening.'

'So you decided to ruin mine instead? Gee—thanks a bunch!' Flora turned to scowl at him in the darkness. 'And you can cut out this running joke about the relationship between Mr Schwartz and myself,' she added grimly. 'I hardly know him, for heaven's sake!'

'That's not how *he* sees it.' Ross drawled as he brought the vehicle to a halt outside the large plantation house. 'In fact, after being bored to death for the past hour, forced to listen to Bernie enumerating your charms, I reckon the guy can only be deeply in love.'

'Ha ha—very funny!' she grated, before recalling that, however much she loathed him, she needed this awful man's help. 'Look, all joking aside—can I rely on you to keep your part of the bargain tonight?'

'What bargain?'

'Oh, come on, Ross—I really don't need any of this nonsense,' she protested as he helped her out of the vehicle. 'I want you to promise *not* to mention the fact that we're still technically married.'

He shrugged his broad shoulders. 'Why should I promise you anything?' he drawled coolly. 'Can you think of one single reason why I shouldn't throw you to the lions tonight? Because I can't.'

'For crying out loud! I'm not asking for the moon. I only want—'

'In fact,' he continued with obvious relish, as she stared at him in dawning horror, 'I reckon it might be quite amusing to watch you being given your just deserts.'

'*My* just deserts...?' she hissed. 'You've got a damned nerve! If anyone ought to get what's coming to them it's *you*—you bastard! You're the one who walked out on me—remember?'

'Oh, yes, I remember only too well!' he ground out harshly. 'I particularly recall the day when I finally saw the light and realised that there was no place for me in your life.'

'That's simply not true!'

'Really...? Well, let's just say that I wasn't prepared to play second fiddle to your job,' he remarked flatly. 'While you, my dear Flora, were clearly prepared to sacrifice everything and everyone to achieve success in your profession.'

'You're not being fair. It wasn't like that!' she lashed back angrily.

'And now here you are. A little older but not much wiser—if your involvement with Bernie Schwartz is anything to go by,' he drawled, coolly ignoring her outburst and the fact that she was clearly trembling with rage. 'I hope you think it's all been worth it?'

Staring up at his tall figure, clearly illuminated by the light spilling out of the wide, open veranda which ran around the old building, Flora would have given everything she possessed to slap that icy, supercilious smile off Ross's handsome face. And the fact that he was looking devastatingly attractive in a white tuxedo only served to increase her fury.

'I suggest that it might be a good idea to remove that scowl from your face,' he drawled mockingly. 'I don't think it will do much for the new Angel Girl's image if she's seen going around with a face like thunder.'

'Oh, *shut up*!' she snapped, before making a supreme effort to try and pull herself together.

She might have known that the double-dealing swine would, if it suited him, happily go back on their deal. But she couldn't just give up at this juncture. She *had* to try and make him see sense.

'Please try and be reasonable,' she said in a calmer tone of voice. 'Even if you hate my guts—and it's quite obvious that you do—it isn't just *me* that's going to be in trouble if you spill the beans. What about the cosmetic company? They've spent a lot of time and money setting up this trip. It really isn't fair of you to throw a spanner in the works at this late stage, is it?'

'Goodness, Flora! Can it be that you're actually thinking about someone else for a change?' he enquired with hard irony.

'Isn't it about time you put on another CD?' she ground out with fury and exasperation. 'I admit that I may have been foolish and silly in the past. But that was *six* years ago, for goodness sake.'

'I'm touched by your concern for ACE,' he drawled. 'But I'm sure that the shareholders of such a large corporation can well afford a small blip on the balance sheet every once in a while. Besides,' he added with a wolfish grin, 'I'm not sure that I can resist the pleasure of seeing that formidable woman, Claudia Davidson, tearing you to shreds!'

'You can't do this to me!' Flora wailed helplessly. 'And why should you be so set on some sort of revenge when you've now got a comfortable life of your own—writing books or whatever?'

'I regard my writing as a business.' His eyes darkened momentarily as he gazed down at her. 'But, this...' he murmured, lifting his hand to run a finger lightly down her cheek. '*This* is definitely personal!'

He was hardly touching her, but the soft brush of his fingers over her skin seemed to be affecting every nerve-end in her trembling body. Backing warily away from the tall figure looming over her, Flora found herself quickly halted by the cold metal frame of the vehicle hard up against her backbone.

'Go away…leave me alone!' she gasped, suddenly feeling breathless and curiously weak at the knees. Which was plainly ridiculous, given that she really, *really* hated this awful man.

'Relax, Flora, we're married—remember?' he taunted, the light spilling out from the house clearly illuminating the gleam of harsh mockery in his eyes as he placed his hands lightly on her shoulders.

'Oh, why…*why* didn't I get a divorce years ago?' she groaned.

'That's interesting—I was just asking myself the same question…' he murmured softly, one hand moving slowly to take hold of her chin, tilting it up towards him so that she was unable to avoid seeing the disturbing glint in his gleaming blue eyes.

'No! Believe me…this really *isn't* the answer,' she protested wildly, unable to prevent herself from quivering at the sudden, fierce heat flooding through her veins, helpless against the ripples of thrilling excitement as his hands slipped down her back and tightened about her slim figure, moulding her quivering body closer to his own hard frame.

But if she'd hoped to escape Flora realised that she had left it far, far too late. His arms were swiftly closing like cruel, fierce bands of steel about her as he lowered his dark head, her muffled protest stifled by the ruthless possession of her lips as his hot, invasive tongue ruthlessly plundering the sweetness within.

It's only a kiss… It's not the end of the world… It's only a kiss…! But, despite rapidly chanting the words to herself—as if, like a mantra, they would somehow preserve her from harm—Flora could feel her senses slipping disastrously out of control.

Their bodies had always fitted each other like a glove, and now she was suddenly transported back in time, the years rolling away as if they'd never existed. Once again the familiar scent of his cologne teased her nostrils, the well-remembered, intimate touch of his hands now slowly relaxing their strong grip to caress her soft curves, the hard strength of the tall, muscular body pressing so closely to her own.

And then she was lost. Lost to all sense of prudence and caution, responding mindlessly to the powerful, sensual excitement spiralling through every fibre of her being. As his kiss deepened she became oblivious to everything except the hard force of his own arousal and the deep thud of his heartbeat, pounding in rapid unison with her own. Consumed by a driving force of dark, passion, drowning in a whirlpool of erotic, sexual desire, she was totally oblivious of everything except a frantic, driving need to respond to the sensual magic of his seductive lovemaking.

And then, with shocking abruptness, Flora found herself being suddenly released. Completely dazed and disorientated, she staggered back to lean helplessly against the vehicle. Dimly, as through a blanket of thick fog, she heard the sound of Ross swearing violently under his breath.

'You're right—that definitely *wasn't* the answer,' he ground out harshly. 'Or, at least, it's not one to which I'm prepared to listen.'

Still feeling totally shattered, Flora couldn't seem to prevent herself from shivering uncontrollably, despite the warmth of the night, as the frenzied heat of desire and passion slowly drained from her body.

'Come on! We can't stay out here all evening,' Ross told her roughly.

'You...er...you go on into the house,' she muttered huskily. 'I...I'll join you as soon as I manage to get my act together...'

He gazed intently down at her bowed head and trembling figure before giving a heavy sigh.

'Relax, Flora—it was only a kiss, for heaven's sake. Not exactly the end of the world. Right?'

'Go away!' she whispered savagely. 'Just go away and leave me alone.'

Ross's dark brows drew together in a deep frown for a moment, and then he shrugged his shoulders. 'OK. But if you haven't joined me within five minutes, I'll be out to collect you. And don't even *think* of trying to run away to avoid this party. Because I'll find you and drag you back here—whether you like it or not. Got the picture?'

Why did he *always* insist on having the last word? But, since she clearly wasn't able to walk anywhere at the moment, let alone run, Flora gritted her teeth and merely nodded her head, taking refuge in what she hoped was a dignified silence.

Waiting until the sound of his footsteps over the gravel faded away, she gave a heavy sigh as she leaned back against the vehicle, staring blindly up at the stars in the night sky. *What in hell was she going to do?*

It was no good trying to pretend that she hadn't been shattered by that torrid embrace just now. Because her aroused body was still twanging like a drum, leaving her feeling totally bereft and almost on the verge of tears. Which, considering that she was now twenty-six years of age, was completely ridiculous.

Ross had always had that effect on her, she told herself with another heavy sigh. Their whirlwind courtship—

meeting and marrying within a few weeks—had hardly been a sensible basis for any long-term relationship. However, while their marriage might have been virtually over almost before it had begun, there'd never been any problem with their sex life. Indeed, she now saw that it had only been the strong bond of mutual attraction which had prolonged the death throes of their relationship. Because even when all else had turned to dust and ashes they had still been able to forget the many quarrels and blistering rows within the shelter and comfort of each other's arms.

Until the day when she returned home to discover that Ross had finally carried out his many threats to leave her.

Over the following years, and especially since her accident, Flora had finally come to see that mere lust and sexual attraction—while necessary ingredients for a successful marriage—were not enough on which to build a lasting relationship; such fierce, sweeping emotions could never be a substitute for true love and unselfish devotion.

However, the realisation of exactly *why* her marriage had failed in the past didn't seem to be of any help to her now. The cruel twist of fate which had brought her to this island—and face to face with Ross after so many years of having been apart from one another—was proving to be a complete disaster. And, to make matters even worse, it seemed that she remained highly susceptible to the dark, magnetic attraction of her ex-husband.

Flora could feel her cheeks burning with shame and embarrassment. It was positively mortifying to have to admit—only privately to herself, of course—that if, just now, instead of swiftly terminating their passionate embrace, her ex-husband had swept her off her feet and into his bed...she wouldn't have been complaining *too* loudly.

Severely shaken by the humiliating discovery that she

was *still* a push-over as far as Ross was concerned, Flora took a deep breath and did her best to pull herself together. So, OK—it wasn't a good scene. But it was hardly the end of the universe. Right? All she had to do was to calm down, stay cool, and make damn sure that she kept well away from Ross's lethal charm.

Unfortunately, saying it was one thing—putting it into practice was quite another, she told herself grimly, brushing a trembling hand over her hair and quickly straightening her dress. However, since Ross was more than likely to carry out his dire threats, she had no choice but to join the party and face the music.

Preoccupied by her own dark thoughts as she walked slowly through the open front door leading into a spacious hall, Flora was startled to find herself being hailed by an old acquaintance.

'Hello, darling!' Keith Tucker, the world-famous American photographer, grinned as he leaned forward to kiss her cheek. 'It seems an age since we last worked together. But I have to say that you're looking as lovely as ever.'

'You're not looking too bad yourself,' Flora grinned, almost sagging with relief to find at least one familiar, friendly face amongst the gathering. She and Keith had often worked together in the past, and although she knew he could be a hard taskmaster they had always been good friends.

'I've been busy looking at various venues for location shots, and wasn't able to be part of the welcoming party earlier this afternoon,' he told her, hailing a passing waiter and placing a drink in her hand. 'Although, since you used to have such wonderful long, straight blonde hair, I'm not sure I would have recognised you even if I *had* been there,' he added with a laugh. 'You look quite different with all these curls.'

'Yes, I know.' Flora shrugged. 'But, thanks to my accident, there's not much I can do about it.'

'What accident....?'

'I was in a bad car smash and they had to shave my head to stitch up all the scalp wounds,' she said, before explaining that it was her long convalescence after the accident which had led to her being off work for so long.

Keith looked at her with concern. 'It sounds as if you've had a hard time.'

'Well, it wasn't exactly a picnic.' She shrugged. 'However, I reckon that I was lucky not to be scarred on the face and so didn't need cosmetic surgery. Unfortunately, when my hair began growing again it turned out to be curly. *Not* exactly the last word in radical chic and total sophistication, I'm afraid,' she added with an ironic grin. 'But, unless I spend a fortune getting it straightened all the time, it looks as if I'm stuck with it.'

'Well...maybe it's not a bad idea to change your image,' Keith murmured, studying her face and hair intently for a moment. 'And—lets's face it—all those curls are going to be *perfect* for this job!'

'Yes, so I've been told.' She sighed, grimacing as he gave a low rumble of laughter. 'Quite honestly, Keith, I've got to the point where I think that if I hear the words "Botticelli angel" once more I'll scream blue murder!'

'Never mind, darling.' He grinned down at her. 'Once we start work—which with any luck will be tomorrow—I'll make sure that Bernie Schwartz is kept well under control.'

'If you can manage that I'll love you for ever!' she quipped.

'Promises...promises!' he murmured dolefully. Which

made her laugh as they both knew that, unlike so many of his gay colleagues, Keith had been happily married for many years to a glamorous ex-model.

'Come along, darling—let's go and join everyone in the other room. I must say that it's a splendid old plantation house,' he murmured. 'I had no idea our host was so wealthy. Maybe I should try my hand at writing thrillers?'

'Don't be such an idiot, Keith!' she laughed.

Still grinning at the thought of such a famous man even thinking of spending his valuable time writing pulp fiction, Flora paused in the shadow of the doorway and gazed around the large living room.

It was only then that it finally came home to her just how far Ross had travelled over the past few years. And not only in terms of distance.

Maybe it was because she'd been so shocked at his sudden reappearance in her life? Or possibly it could be put down to her being affected by tiredness and jet lag...? Whatever the reason, Flora now realised that she really *should* have paid a great deal more attention to Georgie's wild, enthusiastic ravings on the aeroplane concerning her ex-husband's new career as a top-selling author. Because the fruits of his labours were now very plain to see.

Like most of the general public, she'd read plenty of stories in newspapers and magazines about the extraordinarily large sums of money earned by top-selling authors. But it had never occurred to her—not even in her wildest dreams!—that Ross Whitney could now be counted amongst their number.

Staring at the enormous Venetian chandelier casting its sparkling light over the pictures on the walls, at the antique Persian rugs lying on the white marble floor and the huge pieces of wonderfully comfortable, modern Italian furniture, Flora could only shake her head in amazement. She was no expert on modern art, of course, but even *she* was quite capable of recognising paintings by David Hockney and Andy Warhol.

Having done some shows in Milan two years ago, she was also well aware of the simply *astronomical* price tags which would have been attached to the large chairs and sofas scattered around the room. 'Oh, wow! Ross must be worth millions!'

As she gazed around her with open-mouthed astonishment she caught sight of her ex-husband bearing down on her, with Claudia Davidson firmly clutching his arm.

Quickly schooling her expression into one of polite disinterest—she was damned if she'd give Ross the satisfaction or the pleasure of noting her amazement at his new lifestyle—she waited for him to open the batting. Knowing the swine so well, she was *quite* sure he was going to 'tell all'. It was just a matter of where and when.

'Ah…so you managed to find your way over here?' He smiled at her blandly, clearly pretending that he'd never come to fetch her from the cottage.

'Oh, yes, it was no problem,' she murmured with a calm smile, as if she hadn't a care in the world.

He gave a careless shrug. 'That's lucky. I was afraid you might be frightened of stepping on some of the nocturnal creatures to be found in this part of the world. Such as frogs and snakes,' he added with gloomy relish, his lips tightening with annoyance as she gave a trill of light laughter.

'Who, me…? Frightened of some poor little reptiles? Good heavens—whatever gave you that idea?'

'Snakes!' Claudia gave a muffled shriek of horror. 'You don't really have snakes on this island of yours, do you?' She shuddered. 'I can't bear the nasty things!'

I think that's Round One to me! Flora told herself, smiling coldly at Ross, who was forced to quickly reassure the older woman that he'd been only kidding.

'Well, thank goodness for that!' Claudia breathed a sigh of relief. 'Now, I think I need another drink—and I want you to tell me all about your lovely yacht. I hear that it's very, *very* glamorous,' she added, taking a firm grip of his arm and turning to wave imperiously at a waiter.

Raising his glass to Flora, as if acknowledging her brief triumph, Ross flashed her a dangerous, wolfish grin before allowing himself to be led away across the room.

Suddenly feeling mentally and physically exhausted, she leaned for a moment against a nearby wall while the party ebbed and flowed around her. While Keith went off in search of a waiter, to replenish their glasses with more of the delicious rum punch, Flora was grateful for a few minutes' respite from the need for polite conversation.

She was still finding it difficult to come to terms with the evidence, plainly set out before her eyes, that Ross must be a very rich man. It now looked as though he really *did* own this island—something which had seemed so bizarre and ridiculous that she simply hadn't taken it seriously. Which wasn't surprising, she consoled herself, considering that she'd been in such a massive state of shock and horror, right from the moment she'd looked at that book of his on the aeroplane. And ever since then she'd been far too preoccupied to think properly about *anything* other than her own dire problems.

Still…however much she might hate her ex-husband, it would be churlish not to admire his obvious success. When she recalled their first tiny apartment in London, which had been so lovingly furnished with junk shop finds and second-hand pieces of furniture, it was hard not to applaud the hard work and industry which had brought Ross such a long way in such a short space of time.

'Here you are, Flora,' Keith Tucker said as he returned and handed her a glass. 'By the way, you'd better get ready to scream blue murder,' he added with a wry grin. 'Because, unless I'm very much mistaken, it looks as though the Boss Man is making his way over here.'

'Hi, honey...!' a tall, thickset man called out as he ploughed his way across the room towards her.

'I've had about as much of Mr Schwartz as I can stand in one day,' Keith muttered in her ear. 'So I reckon this is where I disappear into thin air.'

'Don't leave me!' she whispered anxiously. But if the wily photographer heard her desperate plea he obviously decided to become temporarily deaf as he faded quickly away into the crowd.

'Hey, Flora—you look *sensational*!' Bernie Schwartz told her loudly, leaning forward to plant a firm kiss on her cheek. 'I'd forgotten just how hot it is down here in the Caribbean,' he added, brandishing a large handkerchief as he wiped the sweat from his forehead beneath a heavy thatch of dark brown hair. 'But, it's just *wonderful* to see you again, honey. Absolutely *great*!'

She smiled politely at the man, whose casual shirt featuring vivid sunsets and palms in day-glo colours of green, red and yellow was particularly hard on the eyes.

However, Flora realised that, while it might be easy to laugh at his lack of dress sense, she owed a great deal to Mr Schwartz. It was, after all, his insistence on her being given the contract with ACE which had led to this job. So, even if it all went down the tubes tonight, she'd always be grateful to the man who'd rescued her career from the doldrums. Besides, she had a gut feeling that it would be a grave mistake not to take him seriously. He couldn't be more than thirty-five years old. And to have achieved his present position in the company Bernie Schwartz must therefore be extremely capable and a force to be reckoned with.

That her instincts were quite correct was quickly and amply demonstrated only a few moments later.

'Hey—I haven't yet introduced you to our new account director for the campaign,' Bernie told her, before adding with a wink, 'I had a bit of a *putsch* in the office last week, and sacked half the staff. Not knowing if they're going to be around to collect next week's pay check, kinda keeps them on their toes!'

'Yes...er...I can see it would,' Flora agreed nervously.

'Damn right!' He chuckled, placing an arm around her slim waist and giving her a squeeze. 'But you and me, honey—we're going to get along just fine. Right?'

'Oh, yes, Mr Schwartz.' She nodded quickly, giving him her best version of a brilliant, megawatt smile. 'Absolutely right!'

'That's my girl!' Bernie laughed, giving her another squeeze as he beckoned to a thin, willowy young man. 'Get yourself over here, Paul,' he called out. 'I want you to meet my very own Botticelli angel.'

'I think Miss Johnson possibly looks more like the *Primavera* in that lovely green dress,' the young man said as he shook Flora's hand.

'Who's this woman, Primy Vera? Have we got her under contract?' Bernie demanded with a frown.

'It...er...it's the name given to one of Botticelli's famous paintings,' Paul muttered. Obviously anxious to extricate himself from a sticky situation, he added nervously, 'It isn't important, sir. Just a joke.'

'I don't like jokes—especially those I don't understand,' Bernie told him, his voice heavy with menace.

'And the amount we're spending on this campaign is *definitely* not funny either!'

'You're one hundred percent right, Mr Schwartz,' Paul agreed fervently.

Luckily, at that point Bernie caught a glimpse of Claudia Davidson across the room. And so, after giving Flora's waist another tight squeeze, he hurried over to have a word with the older woman.

As they watched his departure both Flora and Paul gave a sigh of relief.

'I don't suppose I have to state the obvious,' Paul told her quietly, 'but Mr Schwartz is one very tough cookie.'

'Yes, I had gathered that,' Flora agreed quietly. 'In fact, he's just been telling me that he sacked half his staff the other day.'

Paul sighed. 'I'm grateful for the promotion, of course. Although I suspect it's a job that comes with ulcers attached. However, our firm's very heavily into "reallocation of man-management resources"—or some such jargon.'

'Ah...' She grinned. 'As in: *we* are a team, *you* are overmanned, *they* are redundant?'

'Got it in one!' He laughed, then his expression grew more serious. 'However, all joking aside, it would be as well to keep on the right side of Bernie Schwartz.'

Flora shrugged. 'I'm just out here to do a job. And, as far as I'm concerned, that job does *not* include being over-friendly with Mr Schwartz,' she said firmly. 'So, if he is hoping for a bit of "slap and tickle"—you'd better tell him to look elsewhere.'

She didn't have the opportunity to say any more as Georgie came rushing over with a rather scruffy youth in tow. Quickly introducing the boy as Jamie—Keith

Tucker's young assistant cameraman—she urged Flora to hurry up and join everyone for the buffet supper.

'It's the most glamorous dining room I've ever seen. And as for the food...!' Georgie grinned. 'Just wait till you see some of the delicious puddings. They look really yummy!'

'You're quite right. My housekeeper is famous for her cooking. And especially for her "yummy" puddings!'

At the sudden shock of hearing Ross's deep voice speaking from just behind her left shoulder, Flora nearly jumped out of her skin. Luckily, her startled reaction of confusion and dismay at his sudden reappearance was masked by Georgie's screech of laughter, which drew all eyes to the plump sandy-haired girl.

'Ooh, Ross—I didn't know you were eavesdropping!' Georgie giggled excitedly, her flushed crimson cheeks and expression of blind adoration as she gazed starry-eyed at her host betraying a sudden, wild infatuation for the older man.

Not to mention the fact that the silly girl had drunk far too much rum punch, Flora told herself grimly. But, on second thoughts, maybe Georgie wasn't so foolish? A bit of anaesthetic to get through this awful evening might be just what she, herself, needed...

Quickly following the thought by the deed, Flora swiftly emptied her glass, before realising that she'd made a bad, *bad* mistake as Ross smoothly invited everyone to go and help themselves to the food in the adjacent room.

'While I...' He paused for a moment, before lifting Flora's arm and tucking it firmly in his and going on, 'I, as host, intend to claim the pleasure, and the privilege, of looking after the lovely Miss Johnson.'

'Lucky old you—Claudia will be as sick as a parrot!'

Georgie whispered enviously, before being reluctantly dragged away by the young cameraman.

But Flora would more than willingly have traded places with Georgie—or the fearsome Claudia Davidson—as Ross led her stiff, nervous figure into the spacious dining room.

'I want to make sure that you have a thoroughly enjoyable evening,' he drawled in a cool voice as smooth as silk, before firmly seating her at a table between himself and Bernie Schwartz.

But after one quick, frightened glance at the satanic glint of deep amusement in his hooded blue eyes, Flora had no doubts that if anyone was going to enjoy the rest of the evening it certainly wasn't likely to be her!

CHAPTER FOUR

FLORA groaned as she bent down to open the door of the refrigerator in the tiny but well-equipped kitchen in her cottage.

With trembling hands she removed the ice tray, shaking the cubes onto a small towel before quickly wrapping up the icy parcel and clamping it to her aching head.

Never again! If, as seemed highly unlikely, she actually managed to survive the next few hours, Flora promised herself that she'd never, *ever* again make the mistake of drinking that totally *lethal* concoction, rum punch!

But it wasn't only the after-effects of consuming too much alcohol which was making her feel so sick and nauseous. It was also last night's party, which had been one of the most *ghastly* evenings of her whole life.

In fact, the only mitigating factor in the whole, truly awful scenario had been the phone call from Keith a few moments ago.

Hearing his hoarse whisper down the line, and learning that he, too, had fallen a victim to the demon drink and was therefore cancelling this morning's photo session meant that she could at least lick her wounds in private.

Making her way slowly and carefully across the room on legs that felt as if they were made of cotton wool, she gently lowered herself down into a soft, comfortable chair. So far, so good. Now it was just a case of keeping very, *very* quiet while waiting for the aspirins to take effect and—hopefully—stop that sledgehammer banging away in her head.

When Ross had led her into supper, and insisted on seating her between himself and Bernie Schwartz, it had needed only one quick glance around the table for Flora to know that she was in deep, *deep* trouble. With a sinking heart, she had realised that her ex-husband was clearly planning to extract the maximum amount of fun and amusement from her predicament.

Both Claudia and her faithful shadow, Helen Todd, had obviously been furious to see Flora being given such preferential treatment.

'We don't want this table to become too crowded,' Claudia had announced with ominously tight lips, before turning her needle-sharp baleful gaze on Flora. 'I'm sure Miss Johnson would prefer to join the other young people. Isn't that right, dear?' she'd added with an acid smile.

Unfortunately, despite nodding fervently at Claudia's words, and half-rising from her seat, Flora had found her escape foiled by Bernie Schwartz.

'Just you stay right here, little lady!' he commanded, catching hold of her arm and ignoring the fact that, while a good deal slimmer, she was at least the same height as his thickset figure. 'I want this lovely girl to sit beside *me*,' he said firmly, before turning to glare menacingly at Claudia. 'Do you have a problem with that?'

'Oh, dear me, no!' The older woman gave a nervous trill of laughter. Clearly realising in the nick of time that it was not a good idea to upset the Managing Director of ACE, Claudia quickly gave Flora a totally false, beaming smile. 'In fact, Helen and I were just saying that we hoped you'd be able to join us.'

If she can tell such bare-faced lies it's no wonder the dreadful woman is such a success in business, Flora told herself gloomily, resigned to the fact that, for the time being, she was well and truly stuck with these awful people. Was this going to be the evening from hell—or what?

Grunting with satisfaction at getting his own way, Bernie began steadily drinking his way through a large jug of rum punch, also topping up her glass at every opportunity. The American was obviously enjoying himself no end. And unfortunately he was all over her like a rash.

Ross *must* know that she wasn't romantically interested in Bernie—who clearly fancied himself as a regular Don Juan. And yet he seemed to grow increasingly irritated, drumming his fingers impatiently on the table while the marketing director of ACE conducted a heavy flirtation with his ex-wife.

And she wasn't too thrilled about it either. In fact, although Flora had no alternative but to grit her teeth, smiling modestly at his fulsome compliments, she was definitely *not* amused when Bernie placed his large, hot hand on her thigh.

She really was between the devil and the deep blue sea, Flora told herself with despair. Trying to inch away from Bernie, of necessity she found herself moving closer to Ross. And while her ex-husband merely raised a dark brow in grim amusement at her predicament, Claudia—whose sharp eyes didn't miss a trick—clearly took a very dim view of the way the younger girl was apparently making a play for Ross Whitney. It was a 'no win' situation, and Flora could do little to prevent her rising panic as Bernie placed a firm arm about her waist.

'Stop trying to run away from Uncle Bernie,' he chuckled. 'I wanna tell these good folks, here, that this promotion for our new line of Angel Girl Cosmetics, is going to be the best ever. And do you know why?' He grinned around the table.

'Well, I'll tell you,' he continued as everyone at the table maintained a respectful silence. 'It's all because *I* discovered this lovely girl!' He leaned closer to Flora, planting a smacking wet kiss on her cheek. 'It's her pure, unblemished and truly wholesome quality that's gonna inspire the young kids of today. And when they rush out to buy our wonderful, *wonderful* products—in the hope that they, too, can look as good as this heavenly girl—they're gonna to be spending a hell of a lot of dough. Am I right—or am I right?'

Flora was amazed to hear the cries of 'You're right!' 'So amazingly clever!' and 'Absolutely!' which greeted his bombastic pronouncement. It was only Ross, she noticed, who failed to join in the Greek chorus, merely leaning back in his chair with a bland expression on his face.

Bernie gave a loud chortle of laughter. 'All kidding aside, folks—and, as my assistant Paul will tell you, I *never* joke about business—we're talking *serious* money, here. And it's those mega-bucks which are going to gain me the vice presidency of ACE products!' he added with grim satisfaction. 'So, I'll ask you to raise your glasses, once again, and salute Bernie Schwartz's Botticelli angel!'

Flora stared down at her plate, quite certain that she'd *never* felt so embarrassed and awkward in all her life. Silently praying for a thunderbolt to strike Bernie, before he made her feel any more of a fool than she did already, she became aware that Ross had decided to join in the fun.

'It sounds as if your new line in cosmetics is going to be a great success,' he told Bernie, the mild expression on his face at odds with the dangerous glint of sardonic amusement dancing in his heavy-lidded blue eyes. 'I'm particularly interested in your references to that great

Italian artist, Botticelli. Tell me, have you ever been to *Florence*?'

The heavy emphasis he'd placed on the last word—which, as he knew only too well, was also her original Christian name—suddenly alerted Flora to yet more problems in store for her. She had a nasty suspicion that the embarrassment of the past few minutes was likely to be as nothing when compared to the torment to come.

She was quite right. Clearly unable to resist piling on the agony, Ross proceeded to dominate the conversation. After exhausting the subject of *Florence*, the birthplace of Botticelli, he moved swiftly on to the subject of his next book, which he was planning to set in the Lebanon.

'Beirut is still very much in the news,' he explained. 'And it pays in publishing to go with the *flow*—if you know what I mean?' He turned to smile at Flora, who was having the greatest difficulty in stopping herself from losing all control and slapping the foul man's face.

'Of course, in the old days,' Ross continued, 'Lebanon was always known as the land *flowing* with milk and honey.'

'There ain't much milk and honey around there nowadays,' Bernie commented heavily. And Flora could have hugged the American when he adroitly turned the conversation back to his own particular interest: how to increase the sales of cosmetics.

But Ross wasn't prepared to give up so easily, of course. Oh, no! Having finally exhausted his repertoire of words sounding as near as possible to Flora's original name—including a side-swipe reference to the *flora* and fauna to be found on Buccaneer Island—he then moved on to the subject of marriage.

'Are you married, Bernie?'

'I was. But not any more,' the other man added with a

grim laugh. 'Oh, boy! Did it cost me a packet to get rid of that bimbo or what? Still, things could be worse. At least I'm now foot-loose and fancy-free!' He leered at Flora before turning to Ross. 'How about you, fella? Have you tied the knot yet?'

Flora could feel herself almost choking with rising panic as she, and the other members sitting around the table, waited for Ross's answer.

'Well, yes...' he drawled at last. 'I did tie the knot, as you put it, some years ago. But I untied it again—pretty damn fast!' He gave a heavy, theatrical sigh, shaking his head sorrowfully as he turned to Claudia.

'I guess I was just young and foolish.' He shrugged his shoulders, his mouth trembling slightly as if he was bravely striving to keep a stiff upper lip. 'There I was, totally swept off my feet by a lovely face, but it didn't take me long to discover that I meant nothing to my wife—nothing at all.'

'Oh, no—that's terrible!' Claudia murmured sympathetically.

'A crying shame!' Helen agreed with a heavy sigh.

'Yes, it was very, very hard.' He shook his head sorrowfully. 'She was a model, you know, and very successful. Just like Miss Johnson,' he added, turning to give Flora a brief, unhappy smile. 'Such a success, in fact, that she was always out until late, enjoying herself at parties. While I...I was left on my own, night after night, to pace around our cold, empty house.'

You damned liar! Flora screamed at him silently as the table resounded to warm murmurs of compassion and sympathy.

Glaring at the frightful man, her nails digging painfully into the clenched palms of her hands as she struggled to keep silent, it was all Flora could do not to explode with rage.

What about the hundreds of times Ross had stayed boozing in the pub with his rugby friends while she waited at home with his meal burning to a crisp in the oven? What about the phone calls at midnight—when she'd been worried sick about what might have happened to him— casually explaining that he'd flown off to Scotland or Wales on a job?

'Yes…' Ross gave another deep, heartfelt sigh. 'All I ever wanted was the love of a good woman. Was that *really* too much to ask?'

The swine had obviously chosen the wrong profession, Flora told herself with mounting rage and fury. Forget writing! Her ex-husband would clearly have made a fortune on the stage, if this pathetic 'ham' performance of his was anything to go by.

However, as she glanced at Claudia and Helen she was amazed to see that they'd clearly been taken in by the whole farrago of nonsense. With the glint of tears in their eyes, their bosoms swelling with indignation at the way Ross had been maltreated by his wicked wife, they leaned sympathetically across the table, only *too* anxious to console the tall, dark and handsome man.

The poor, deluded fools! Little do they know what a *rat* the man really is, Flora thought viciously, jabbing a fork into a piece of chicken on her plate, and wishing that she had a long, sharp, deadly stiletto—plus the opportunity to plunge it deep into her ex-husband's black heart.

'What about you, Flora?'

'Wh-what…?'

Preoccupied with her own grim thoughts, Flora realised that she'd foolishly lowered her guard and allowed herself to become careless.

'I...er...I'm sorry, I didn't quite catch what you said...?' she muttered in breathless panic, playing for time as she frantically tried to think of an answer to the next question, which she knew would be coming any minute.

Unfortunately Ross did not disappoint her.

'I was just wondering about your marital status...?' he drawled smoothly.

'I...er...I don't quite know what you mean?' she muttered evasively.

Her hands tightly clenched together, she stared down at her plate in despair. Ross had cleverly boxed her into a corner, and there seemed nothing she could do to save herself. It was no good trying to fib her way out of this situation. Goodness knows, she'd *already* told enough white lies to ice a cake! Flora reminded herself with rising hysteria. So, deliberately misleading everyone here this evening would only make matters far, far worse when the truth finally came out.

'Come along, Miss Johnson—there's no need to be shy. I was merely asking whether you're a married woman.' Ross, clearly determined to have his pound of flesh, smiled blandly around the table. 'I'm sure we'd all *love* to hear the answer to that question.'

'Well...the fact is...'

'The fact is that Miss Johnson is not married,' Claudia announced loudly. 'Nor is she likely to be for at least the next three years. *Not* if she wishes to complete her contract,' the older woman added grimly, before turning her hard gaze on the strangely pale, ashen face of the girl sitting across the table. 'That's right, isn't it, dear?'

'Oh, yes—I definitely *do* want to complete my contract,' Flora breathed, nodding frantically and almost sagging with relief at being rescued from her dire predicament—and without having to tell a deliberate lie. Maybe Claudia wasn't really quite so awful, after all?

'It's very important to ensure that there's no breath of scandal about our model,' Helen Todd chimed in, clearly determined to ensure their host realised that Flora was definitely 'off limits' as far as he was concerned.

Claudia nodded vigorously. 'Helen's quite right,' she told Ross. 'Our campaign is designed to promote a concept of fresh, natural and unsullied femininity. So, our Angel Girl must be seen to be pure in thought *and* deed.'

Bernie Schwartz, clamping his arm around Flora's waist once more, dragged her closer to him as he whispered hoarsely in her ear, 'Not *too* pure, I hope! Not as far as Uncle Bernie is concerned. Right?'

Would this awful evening *never* end? Flora asked herself desperately. It was as though she was being squeezed, like the filling of a sandwich, between Ross—continually asking difficult questions which he knew she had no hope of answering—and Bernie—who was clearly a well-paid-up member of the Wandering Hands Society.

Trembling with tiredness and mental exhaustion, she was almost getting to the point of jumping to her feet, and screaming, *Yes, I'm married to the foul swine sitting beside me! Cancel my contract immediately—I want to go home*! when she was saved at the eleventh hour by Ross, who at last brought her torment to a close.

'I hope you will all continue to enjoy yourselves,' he said, rising from his chair. 'But it's clearly time that this young lady hit the sack.'

Taking no notice of Bernie's loud protests, he almost dragged Flora's shrinking figure to her feet, politely but firmly making his excuses as he led her from the room.

She was just too tired and weary to put up more than a token fight when, after leaving the plantation house, she found herself swept off her feet by Ross and dumped in the passenger seat of his Land Rover. It was only on arriving back at her cottage, a few minutes later, that she eventually found her voice.

'Thanks for *nothing*!' she ground out as he unlocked the front door of the little house. 'I hope you're pleased with yourself for putting me through hoops tonight. Because it has to be *the* worst experience of my entire life! Haven't you anything better to do with your time? Apart from writing those rubbishy novels of yours, of course,' she added spitefully.

By the light of the vehicle's blazing headlamps she could see his lips tighten at her scathing description of his books.

'There's no need to sound quite so hysterical,' he drawled in a hateful, mocking tone of voice. 'Especially when I was merely trying to make a contribution to this evening's enjoyment.'

'A contribution to this evening's *what*?' she hissed savagely, almost beside herself with fury as she glared incredulously up at him. 'Believe me—your most helpful "contribution" would be to stop breathing!'

'Hey—relax!' He grinned, his shoulders shaking with suppressed laughter. 'It was only a tease. A bit of harmless fun and amusement, that's all.'

'I'll give you "harmless fun and amusement",' she shrieked, a cloudy red mist filling her vision as she finally lost all control, drumming her tightly clenched fists on his broad chest—and any other part of his anatomy that she could reach.

'Now Flora—calm down!' he commanded, wincing as she landed a well-aimed blow on his shin with her spiky high-heeled sandal.

'Calm down? Hah—I haven't even started yet!' she

panted. 'I'll kill you… I'll make you wish you'd never been born! I'll…'

'*Cool it!*' he growled, swiftly catching hold of her flailing wrists in a vise-like grip while with the other hand he opened the door. Quickly switching on the lights, he swept her protesting figure up in his arms and strode rapidly towards the bedroom.

'Put me down at once—you rat!' she stormed, frantically wriggling in a vain effort to escape.

'With pleasure!' he retorted grimly, tossing her lightly down onto the bed.

'I've had quite enough of this nonsense,' he continued as she lay, winded and breathless, gazing muzzily up at his tall figure. 'You're clearly in no fit state to listen to reason at the moment. So, I suggest that we leave all discussion of your problems to the morning, when you'll have had a good night's sleep and will be—hopefully!— a good deal more sober.'

'Come back here!' she stormed as he turned on his heel and quickly left the room. 'I haven't finished with you yet. Not…not by a long chalk.'

But, after finally managing to scramble off the bed, cursing her legs which appeared to be unaccountably wobbly as she staggered unsteadily across the floor, Flora discovered that the swine was running out on her once again. Ross's only answer being a sardonic laugh followed by a loud bang as he slammed the front door shut behind him.

Leaning helplessly against the wall, she'd felt certain that her head was about to explode with rage and fury. There had seemed nothing she could do to prevent stinging, angry tears of acute frustration trickling down her cheeks as she'd listened to the sound of Ross's vehicle fading into the distance.

All through the long, hot night—during which she'd

felt so ill, convinced that each breath would be her last—
there had been only one thought in her sore head. She
must try and find a way of escaping—both from her ex-
husband and from the horrific, fiendish nightmare in
which she now found herself.

Unfortunately, as Flora, now glumly pressing ice cubes
to her head, was forced to admit, she was well and truly
stuck. Nothing other than collapsing with a full-blown
nervous breakdown and being carted off to the loony bin
was going to get her out of this fix—and off this damn
island. Although, from the way she felt at the moment, it
wouldn't be long before she really *was* checking in at the
funny farm.

It might have been tempting, last night, to wallow in a
positive ocean of self-pity—convinced that it would serve
Ross right if she *did* flip her lid and was subsequently
locked up in an asylum. Now, however, in the cold light
of day, it was obvious that her lousy ex-husband had just
been having fun at her expense—and would only laugh if
she did become as nutty as a fruitcake. So, why give him
the satisfaction? Wasn't it about time she started fighting
back?

Busy trying to think of ways in which she could make
Ross's life difficult—or at least sufficiently uncomfortable
to persuade him to leave her strictly alone—Flora realised
that she was, at last, beginning to feel a bit better.
Unfortunately, no sooner had she become convinced that
she might actually live to fight another day when she was
startled to hear a loud knocking on the door.

Oh, no! There was only one person who was likely to
be up this early in the morning, bright-eyed and bushy-
tailed. Her rotten ex-husband, that was who!

Flora ground her teeth with fury. Well, she simply
wasn't going to answer the door—and that was that! But,

eventually succumbing to the repeated rat-a-tat-tat, she groaned helplessly as she forced herself to her feet before striding angrily across the room.

'I thought I told you to get the hell out of my life!' Flora rasped as she jerked open the door.

However, as her eyes adjusted to the painfully bright light of a Caribbean morning, she realised that the figure standing on her doorstep wasn't Ross, after all.

'Oh...um...hello Georgie,' she muttered lamely, her face suddenly flaming crimson with embarrassment. 'What...er...what can I do for you?'

'I'm sorry to be such a nuisance, but I wonder if I could borrow some sun cream?'

Flora gazed at the beads of perspiration trickling down the plump, flushed cheeks of the girl standing in the doorway and gave a heavy sigh.

'You're right! I've been a complete idiot,' Georgie confessed with an embarrassed grin. 'But, I simply *daren't* tell Claudia and the others that I forgot to buy any sun lotion before we left London. Not when we're working for a cosmetic company. They'd probably fire me on the spot!'

Flora hesitated for a moment, briefly tempted to tell the silly girl to get lost, because she had more than enough problems of her own to cope with. However, after another glance at Georgie's pale, freckled skin—which, unprotected, would swiftly burn to a crisp beneath the hot sun— she realised that she had no choice.

'OK.' She shrugged. 'You'll have to excuse the mess, because I haven't had a chance to tidy up this morning. But come on in and I'll see what I can find.'

'Are you sure that it's all right?' Georgie looked at her quizzically. 'I mean, it sounded as if you were expecting someone...?'

'No…no—absolutely not,' she muttered, inwardly cursing herself, yet again, for having been so careless. Georgie was obviously an incurable gossip. And with the other girl's nose now twitching, like a truffle hound on the trail of a delicious morsel, she was obviously going to have to come up with some excuse for answering the door so aggressively.

'I…um…I have to confess that I was an idiot yesterday evening, and drank far too much rum punch.'

'Didn't we all?' Georgie groaned in sympathy. 'I was up half the night—so was my room-mate—and we've both decided to become completely teetotal for at least a week.'

'Yes, well…I was feeling like death warmed up, and I guess I…um…I must have nodded off for a moment, completely forgetting where I was…' Flora improvised quickly. 'Just a bad dream—you know how it is?'

'Nightmares are awful,' Georgie agreed sympathetically, appearing to lose interest in the subject as she followed Flora's slim figure through the large, cool sitting room and into the bedroom.

'These guest cottages are really sweet, aren't they?' she continued. 'The one I'm sharing with the hair and make-up girl, Sarah Roberts, is decorated in sunshine-yellow. But I just *love* this bluey-green colour scheme.'

'Yes, it's very nice,' Flora muttered, hunting through her make-up bag for a tube of total sun block.

'In fact, everything about this island is really great!' Georgie continued enthusiastically as she sat down on the bed, gazing about her with interest. 'Not to mention Ross too, of course! He's not at all stand-offish, is he? I thought that such a famous best-selling author would be far too grand to speak to lowly worms like myself. But he's really nice and friendly.'

Flora gave a weary sigh, wishing to heaven that she'd been hard-hearted and kept her mouth shut. After the last traumatic twenty-four hours, all she wanted was to be left entirely alone. Unfortunately, it looked as if this girl was determined to settle down for a good gossip.

'The photograph of Ross on the cover of his book was pretty yummy—but I reckon he's *far* more gorgeous in the flesh. I'm absolutely mad about him. A real case of "sex on legs"!' Georgie giggled. 'What do you think?'

'I think that I'd sell my soul for a cool shower—*and* total peace and quiet,' Flora retorted grimly as she at last found what she was looking for. Handing the tube to the other girl, she added with a weary, apologetic smile, 'I'm sorry to be such a grouch, but I'm still feeling deathly ill. Maybe we can get together later?'

'You're right...I'm not feeling too good myself. And I suppose I ought to take it easy this morning,' Georgie acknowledged as she rose reluctantly to her feet. 'Oh, by the way, did you notice Claudia and Helen last night?'

'No,' Flora lied, determined not to be drawn into a discussion about the horrid women which, if she gave Georgie half a chance, was likely to last some hours.

'Well...I nearly *died* trying not to laugh. They were both almost foaming at the mouth with middle-aged lust! I've never seen anything so pathetic. Sarah tells me that they're *really* excited because they've heard that although Ross was married to someone in the past, he's currently unattached. So, it looks as if they reckon he's up for grabs!'

'I can only wish them the very best of luck,' Flora muttered grimly.

'Oh—come on! Those old wrinklies haven't a hope in hell,' Georgie retorted scornfully. 'Besides, his girlfriend is due to arrive here, either today or tomorrow. Which will *really* put their noses out of joint!'

'His girlfriend?'

'Yes, you know—Lois Shelton.'

'Who…?'

'Honestly, Flora! Where have you been living for the past few years? On Mars?' The plump girl gave a hoot of laughter. 'Even if you've never read any of Ross's books, you *must* have heard of Lois Shelton. The well-known actress, with flaming red hair and a really *amazing* figure…?' Georgie prompted. 'She starred in *Moment of Truth* and *Portrait of a Lady*.'

Flora frowned for a moment, before slowly nodding her head. While she hadn't remembered the film star's name, she now had no difficulty in recalling the actress's lovely face and, as Georgie had so rightly pointed out, her amazing figure.

'Anyway, Lois has just won an Oscar for her part in the film *Fear No Evil*,' Georgie continued enthusiastically. 'It hasn't come out in Britain yet, but I'm told it's really great. Ross also got an Oscar for adapting the screenplay from his book, which was a *mega* bestseller.'

Flora frowned. 'How did you learn about this?'

'Well, I've always been mad about films,' the other girl grinned. 'And I noticed Lois in her first major film, *Ring of Destiny*. It was only a small part, of course, but even then you could see that she had lots of talent.'

'No…er…I meant how did you hear that this actress was Ross's girlfriend?' Flora murmured casually. Georgie laughed. 'Oh, that's easy. The newspapers and magazines have been full of their torrid romance. They were on location together,' she added, as if that explained everything.

'Oh, right.' Flora turned away to pick up a dress, busy

placing it carefully on a hanger as she murmured, 'Did you say that Lois Shelton is arriving here soon? Are you quite sure about that?'

'Well, that's the rumour I heard last night.' Georgie shrugged as she made her way across the room. 'She's fantastically beautiful, of course, which is really going to put a spoke in Claudia and Helen's wheels—I'm happy to say!'

'Hmmm...' Flora murmured in vague agreement, wondering why her headache had now returned with a vengeance.

'But even if Lois Shelton doesn't turn up I reckon those two triumphs of the embalmer's art are going to be way out of luck,' Georgie told her. Popping her head back around the door, she added with a grin, 'Because I noticed, even if *they* didn't, that Ross has hardly taken his eyes off *you*—right from the moment we landed on this island!'

'Goodbye, Georgie!' Flora ground out, slamming the door shut behind the other girl's plump figure before staggering across the room and throwing herself face-down onto the bed.

Well, what did you expect? Flora asked herself roughly, some time later, as she stood beneath the cool needle-spray of the shower. Ross was now successful, rich and as handsome as ever. So he was bound to have any amount of beautiful, stunningly attractive girlfriends at his beck and call. Quite honestly, it would be far more amazing if he hadn't. And why should you care, anyway? she asked herself defiantly. Especially since, if Ross was going to be busy making love to Lois Shelton, he wouldn't have any time to plague the life out of his ex-wife.

Despite trying to see the bright, positive side of Georgie's news about the imminent arrival of the glamorous film-star, Flora couldn't seem to throw off a feeling of deep depression. Even telling herself that she was merely suffering from a hangover and that it was perfectly normal to feel low on looking back at a failed marriage didn't seem to help.

They'd both been very ambitious, Flora reminded herself as she turned off the shower before slowly towelling herself dry. And that had been the trouble, of course. With two young, headstrong and ambitious personalities, both striving to succeed in their various careers, it wasn't surprising that they'd had such an explosive relationship. Or, when it came to the crunch, that they should each have expected the other partner to fall in with their individual plans.

Until a year ago it had never occurred to Flora even to question her choice of career as a fashion model. But following that horrendous car accident, which had resulted in such a long stay in hospital followed by an even longer convalescence, she'd had plenty of time in which to realise just what a mess she'd made of her life so far.

It hadn't been easy facing up to the brutal truth—that she'd been mostly to blame for the break-up of her marriage. Now, of course, she could see that she'd been an idiot. Because no career was worth the sacrifice of a marriage. But, being fiercely independent at the time, she hadn't been prepared to put her job and considerable earnings on the back burner when Ross had been offered that post in South America.

Still…maybe it would have all ended in tears even if she *had* agreed to accompany Ross aboard? Even allowing for the old maxim that a brief, whirlwind courtship was hardly the best basis for a life-long relationship, Flora had come to see that both she and Ross had been far too young, each far too determined on having their own way, for their life together to have had any chance of success.

However, by the time she'd fully recovered her strength after the accident, if she had been able to earn a reasonable living in any other profession she'd have grabbed the opportunity to do so. Unfortunately, having run away from both home and school at such a young age, she was singularly ill-equipped to do anything other than pose for the camera. And, despite being by then heartily sick and tired of such a boring, vacuous way of life, she hadn't been able to come up with any other way of earning her living.

Trying to be ruthlessly honest as she slipped into a pair of pale blue shorts and a matching T-shirt, Flora wondered if the reason she was feeling so low was nothing more than a case of jealousy. Not of his girlfriend, of course, she quickly assured herself. Absolutely not! But maybe she was guilty of the sin of envy? Could she be subconsciously resenting the fact that Ross was now so rich and successful…?

Deep in thought, Flora was startled to hear, once again, a loud knocking on her front door. Not Georgie, yet again?

But, as she'd told herself earlier, she ought to have known *exactly* who'd be outside her door this early in the morning.

'What do you want?' she demanded, scowling up at the mocking, sardonic grin on the face of her ex-husband.

'I thought it was time we had a long talk.'

'Forget it!' she snapped.

'So, I've come to take you out for a drive,' he continued, ignoring her words and easily frustrating her attempt to slam the door in his face. 'I know,' he added firmly over her protests, 'I'm well aware that the Angel Girl must be kept out of the sun. However, I have a shady spot in mind. And you'd better bring your swimsuit in case you feel like cooling off in my pool later.'

'I'm not going *anywhere* with you!'

Ross shrugged. 'You can come willingly—or I'll drag you out by force,' he drawled. 'It's all the same to me.'

'I just bet it is—you bully!' she ground out angrily. But his only reply was a quite maddening rumble of sardonic laughter.

Furious, she scowled up at him as she realised that, unless someone was going to come to her rescue within the next few seconds, she didn't have any choice but to do his bidding.

A few minutes later, her slim figure rigid with anger, she was slamming the front door loudly behind her.

Heaven knows, Flora told herself as she stalked down the steps of the veranda towards the Land Rover, she'd always hated violence of any sort. All the same, it was highly disturbing to realise just how many nasty, vicious and downright bloodthirsty thoughts she'd had in the last twenty-four hours. In fact, she was now *quite* capable of understanding just what it was that drove some people to commit murder!

CHAPTER FIVE

DETERMINED to both look and act as if she had absolutely no interest in their destination, Flora couldn't help frowning in puzzlement when Ross eventually brought the open-topped Land Rover to a halt.

'What on earth is this place? And what are we doing here?' she demanded, staring up at an extremely large wooden shed overlooking a wide stretch of golden sand edging the ocean.

As she gazed at the scene before her Flora noticed that the structure was poised over a narrow inlet which seemed to have been carved out of the beach, allowing sea water to flow freely towards the far end of the large, rectangular building.

'It's a boathouse. I normally keep my yacht here during the hurricane season,' Ross told her. 'Or when I'm likely to be away from the island for any length of time—like my recent trip to America.'

'I thought we were supposed to be having a "long talk".' She gazed at him accusingly. 'You always were as artful as a cage full of monkeys. But I'm a lot wiser now—and there's *no way* I'm going sailing with you!'

'I never said—'

'Forget it!' she told him tersely, still feeling highly aggrieved at having being virtually kidnapped by her ex-husband. And the fact that he was looking diabolically attractive in a dark blue open-necked T-shirt—not to mention those white shorts practically glued to his slim hips—wasn't doing anything to improve her bad temper either.

'For heaven's sake, Flora—stop being such a grouch!'

'I don't care if I *am* being grouchy,' she muttered peevishly. 'Because I haven't forgotten almost drowning the last time you took me out in a leaky old boat even if you have.'

'Hey, come on—that was years ago!' Ross grinned. 'Besides, I'd only been lent that old schooner, so I was hardly responsible for the fact that it wasn't seaworthy. I can assure you that my present boat is as safe as houses.'

'Oh, yeah...?' She gave a snort of derisive laughter. 'Well, even if you aren't too bothered about your own life-span—I'm not yet ready for a watery grave. In fact, I've no intention of *ever* going sailing with you again. And that's that!'

'Who said anything about going for a sail?' Ross drawled coolly. Jumping out of the vehicle, he began striding towards the boathouse. 'Stop bellyaching—we haven't got all day,' he added as he unlocked the door before disappearing inside the large wooden structure.

It only took a moment for Flora to realise that Ross—the sneaky rat!—had carefully removed the car keys from the ignition. And with no immediate prospect of escape in view she could only give a heavy sigh as she trailed slowly and reluctantly after him.

Fully expecting the interior to be dark and dingy, she was surprised to find the large building flooded with light. This was clearly due to the fact that the huge wooden doors at the far end were wide open and framing a view of sparkling waves beneath an azure sky.

Never having been inside a boathouse before, Flora was also surprised to note that the wooden structure was merely a shell enclosing a concrete dock filled with sea water—whose waves slapped gently and rhythmically against the sides of a large, elegant sailing yacht.

Making her way gingerly along the narrow, slatted wood walkway which ran around the edge of the building, she saw Ross busy coiling some ropes on the deck of the boat, which towered above her.

'You'll be glad to hear that I've got some coffee on the boil,' he told her with a grin, before moving across to an open hatchway and disappearing out of sight.

'Well, at least you've got something right!' she muttered, grumbling beneath her breath as she clambered aboard the boat and cautiously negotiated the narrow steps leading down into the main cabin.

'How do you like your coffee these days? With cream and sugar?'

'Just black, please,' she murmured, looking around the cabin.

Although unexpectedly large and roomy, with two long, wide, comfortable seats on either side of a table, the various fixtures and fittings of the main cabin were definitely not what she'd have called 'luxurious'.

Thanks to her job, which often called for exotic locations, Flora had been on several yachts belonging to wealthy millionaires, most of which seldom seemed to leave their safe, comfortable berths for the open sea. However, this was clearly the boat of a man who took his sailing seriously—preferring to spend his money on important items of marine equipment and not particularly interested in mere decoration.

'Well! If this is the glitzy, glamorous yacht which that awful woman, Claudia, was yakking on about last night she's certainly in for one big surprise.' Flora gave a caustic laugh. 'Incidentally, if you want to take *her* out and drown her—that's just fine by me!'

'I already know what a bitch you can be, Flora—so, there's no need to try and prove it!' He glared angrily at her. 'However, while it's obvious that you've got a mammoth hangover, I'm not prepared to listen to any more gripes. So, pull yourself together and stop sulking. *Right?*'

'All right...all right,' she muttered. 'Maybe I was a bit nasty about Claudia, but...'

'And if you're really all that interested in my yacht—which, as you can see, is certainly *not* the floating gin palace of your and Claudia's heated imagination—you'll be glad to hear I've no intention of going sailing today. OK?'

'OK...I'm sorry. You've made your point. There's no need to go bananas,' she grumbled, sinking down onto one of the wide leather seats and wondering why men seemed to get so upset by any criticism of either their cars or their boats.

'Although you're quite right about the hangover,' she admitted with a heavy sigh as he handed her a steaming mug of coffee. 'What in the heck did you put in those rum punches last night?'

He shrugged. 'Only the best Jamaican rum. Unfortunately, it seems to have carved a swathe through the ranks of ACE. However, if it's any consolation,' he added with a grin, 'you're in better shape than most of your companions. I'm sorry to say that your boyfriend, Bernie, is in a *really* bad way!'

'How many times do I have to tell you that he's *not* my boyfriend?' She scowled up at her ex-husband. 'And if he's got a bad headache—anything like the one I woke up with—it serves him right! The man was a perfect pest.'

'Oh, come on, honey—there's no need to be so hard on poor old Uncle Bernie...'

'Now who's being bitchy?' she muttered grimly as
Ross mimicked her employer's nasal twang.

'Touché!' He laughed, before adding more seriously,
'It's too early in the day to quarrel, Flora. How about a
non-aggression pact—for the next few hours at least?'

'Well…that might not be a bad idea,' she agreed cautiously. 'But I'm still waiting to hear why you've dragged
me halfway across this island of yours?'

Ross shrugged his broad shoulders. 'I'd originally
thought of taking you scuba diving. But, since you've
obviously still got some alcohol in your bloodstream, I
think we'd better go snorkelling instead. And before you
start moaning and groaning, yet again,' he added firmly
as she opened her mouth to protest, 'I merely want to
show you a particularly colourful, shallow coral reef, only
a few hundred yards away from here. OK?'

Beware the Greeks bearing gifts, Flora told herself,
gazing searchingly up at his tanned face. But as he explained that the reef was one of the reasons why he'd
bought the island she couldn't help but detect the note of
sincerity in his voice. Especially when he outlined the
problems affecting coral due to ever-increasing pollution
of the world's seas and oceans.

'It's no great shakes, of course,' Ross admitted with a
slight shrug. 'But I like to think that the steps I'm taking
to protect the reefs around Buccaneer Island are going
some way to helping the cause.'

'Well…OK,' she agreed slowly as he filled a Thermos
with coffee before removing the snorkelling equipment
from a locker. In fact, if she was honest, Flora knew that
she'd love nothing better than to be able to immerse herself in the cool, refreshing waters of the Caribbean sea.

A few minutes later, as she followed Ross's tall figure
through a grove of palm trees edging the ocean, she re-

called the last time they'd been snorkelling and scuba diving together.

It had been just at the point when their marriage was finally cracking up. All the same, during that brief holiday in the Maldives—well away from the strain and tensions of everyday life—they'd managed to put all their differences aside. It had been an idyllic, carefree time, in which they'd spent most of their days exploring the many reefs around the island on which they'd been staying. But if she'd hoped that it would herald a new and happier phase in their relationship Flora was to find that she'd been doomed to disappointment. Because only one month later Ross had walked out of both her life and their marriage.

However, there was nothing to be gained by recalling past unhappiness, Flora told herself firmly as Ross came to a halt beneath the shade of some sweet-smelling Tamarind trees, overshadowed by tall palms at the edge of the beach.

Watching as he spread out a tartan rug before undoing a canvas duffel bag containing the snorkels, she was glad that she'd had the sense, back at her cottage, to change into a bikini beneath her shorts and T-shirt. Because she really didn't fancy having to search for some shelter and privacy before struggling out of her clothes. And certainly not in front of her ex-husband!

'Keep your sneakers on,' he called out, his words muffled as he stripped off his dark blue cotton pullover. 'Not only do some of the sea urchins have toxic spines, but the coral is very sharp and can cut your feet to ribbons.'

'I...er...I hadn't thought of that. Thanks for the warning,' she muttered, quickly removing her own shorts and T-shirt and taking a deep breath as she tried to ignore the sight of his wide, broad shoulders and deeply tanned chest, liberally sprinkled with dark curly hair.

Why on earth couldn't he wear those fashionable loose swimming shorts like everyone else? Because if there wasn't a law against allowing attractive men to swan around practically naked there damn well should be! Flora told herself grimly, her cheeks flushing as she quickly averted her gaze from his long bronzed legs, topped by a pair of scandalously brief black swimming trunks.

What was more, it was absolutely maddening to note his deep tan. It's all right for *him* she fumed, only too well aware of her own pale alabaster skin, which she was forced to keep well out of the sun. *He* doesn't have to go around looking white and sickly, like some victim of the vampire—a startling contrast, out here in the Caribbean, to any normal girl's healthy tan.

So what if I look a fright? So who cares? she told herself defiantly, quickly adjusting a bow at the front of her pale green bikini.

'It's still early in the day,' Ross told her, squinting up at the morning sun. 'But as we're going to be snorkelling you'd better protect your back and shoulders.'

'I've already thought of that,' she told him with a brittle smile, before taking a can of oily sun screen from her bag. 'It won't take me a minute to—'

'I'll do that,' he said, quickly taking the can from her hand.

'Hey! What do you think you're doing?' she snapped. 'I'm perfectly capable of spraying myself—thank you very much!'

'Whoa…relax!' he drawled quietly, before covering her back in a fine mist. 'What's got into you this morning? You never used to be this jumpy.'

'It must be the hangover,' she muttered nervously, ashamed to find herself shivering involuntarily at the touch of his warm hand moving gently over her shoulders.

'And in any case the whole point of the spray is that there's no need to rub the stuff in.'

He laughed. 'Ah—but that takes away half the fun, doesn't it?'

'Not as far as I'm concerned,' she retorted, quickly spinning around and grabbing the can from his hand. 'So, go away and play your "fun" games with someone else, Ross. Because, while I may be a blonde, I'm certainly not dumb!'

'How very true,' he agreed with a sardonic grin. 'Maybe "super aggressive" might be a better description, hmm?'

'Thanks a bunch!' She glared up at him. 'Now, are we going snorkelling together—or not?'

'Well...' he drawled, pausing as his eyes roamed slowly over her long, slim body. 'I suppose there are worse ways to pass the time. What do you think?'

'You *really* don't want to hear what I think!' she snapped, quickly snatching up her snorkel and striding down across the sand towards the sea, her rigidly angry figure followed by the sound of his ironic laughter.

However, after plunging into the rolling waves, Flora quickly discovered that the cool, refreshing sea water was sweeping away all trace of bad temper. Swimming slowly behind Ross as he led the way along a narrow, deep trench, she was far too enchanted by the sight of the coral reef, teaming with sea life, to waste her time being angry with her ex-husband.

Watching, enchanted, as shoals of tiny fish swam in and out of the knobbly coral, Flora was amazed at the brilliant colours of the bright pink rose anemones, the blue sea slugs and the green, pink and purple sea urchins whose fronds waved gently to and fro in the current.

But all good things must come to an end, and she nodded as Ross tapped her on the shoulder before leading the way back down the trench towards the shore.

'That was really *fantastic!*!' Flora sighed happily a few minutes later as he handed her a towel to dry her hair. 'How did you come to buy this island?'

'Oh, the usual way one buys anything, these days—although, to be technically accurate, I've leased the island from the Government of Antigua,' Ross drawled as he poured them both a mug of coffee. 'However, I think money came into it somewhere along the line.'

'Yes, I imagine it must have done,' she agreed dryly, sitting down on the rug beside him.

'Money—and a lot of luck, of course,' he mused quietly.

'Luck?'

He shrugged. 'Nobody really knows what causes a book to become a bestseller. You can have a really well-written, terrific story—plus all the hype in the world—and it can still turn out to be a dud. Which means that very few authors manage to hit the big time. So, if I hadn't struck lucky with my books it's highly unlikely that I'd be sitting here today.'

'I didn't realise that it was such a precarious profession,' she said, buried in thought for a moment as she slowly sipped her coffee. 'Although I hope you won't mind me saying that I...well, I'm still having difficulty coming to terms with the fact that you're now a well-known author.'

'As it happens, so am I!' he told her with a wry grin. 'I never imagined that my books would take off so fast, or be so successful. Never in a million years.'

'But what made you decide to start writing in the first place? I don't recall you ever mentioning that you wanted to be an author. Certainly not when you were married to me, anyhow.'

'And would you have listened, if I had?' He lifted a dark, quizzical eyebrow.

'Of course I would.'

'Well, as I remember, I *did* try to talk to you about wanting to write a book,' he told her flatly. 'But, as usual, you were far too involved in your own career.'

'That's simply not true!' she protested. 'I have absolutely *no* recollection of any conversation with you about your ambition to be an author. I'll admit that I'm not a great reader of thrillers. Mainly because I'm not too keen on books dealing with blood and violence. But if I'd known that you *seriously* wanted to write I'd have done all I could to help.'

'Oh, really?'

'Come on, Ross—be fair! You *know* I would.'

He shrugged. 'Maybe I didn't stress how important it was to me. And, if I'm honest, I might have felt that you'd either laugh or pour cold water on the idea.' He remained deep in thought for a few moments, before giving a heavy sigh. 'So many people say that they want to write a book. But in fact very few actually achieve their ambition. Sometimes it's because they lack the courage to go for it. But mostly it's because their lives are so busy that they can't find either the time or the opportunity to do so. And I would never have been able to take the gamble if it hadn't been for my father.'

'What's your father got to do with it?' Flora turned to frown at him. 'I thought you couldn't stand him, and—'

'No, that was my stepfather,' Ross corrected her quickly. 'And you're right. I always loathed the man who took my real father's place—although I have to admit that he made my mother very happy. I was undoubtedly a difficult teenager when my mother married again, and, after some explosive rows, I went back to live with my grandmother, who'd looked after us when Dad left home. Do you remember Gran?'

Flora nodded. She certainly hadn't forgotten the grim-faced, starchy old lady who'd died just a few months after their wedding. Granny Whitney had clearly been a holy terror, and as tough as old boots. But Ross had been devoted to the woman who'd brought him up following his parents' divorce when he was only a few years old.

'Gran was determined that I should train to be a mining engineer. It was no good telling her that I wanted to be a writer.' Ross turned to give Flora a wry smile. 'She used to say, "It's the Royal School of Mines for you, my lad. Because if it was good enough for your father it's good enough for you." But my heart was never really in it.'

'But I don't understand how your real father comes into the story?'

Ross lay back on the rug, placing his hands beneath his dark head as he stared up at the leafy fronds of the tall palm trees, silhouetted against the blue sky.

'After he and my mother divorced, Dad went off to the Middle East, and we only met on the very few occasions when he returned to England. I can't say I ever really knew him,' Ross added with a heavy sigh. 'But soon after you and I split up I heard that he'd died and left me quite a lot of money. Which meant that I could afford to give up work, for a few years at least, and try my luck at writing.'

'Well, it certainly looks as if the gamble was worth it. And I was *very* pleased to hear of your success,' Flora told him brightly, determined that he shouldn't suspect her of being ungenerous, or suffering from a case of sour grapes.

PLAY "LUCKY HE
AND YOU GET . . .

★ **Exciting Harlequin romance no**

★ **PLUS a Lovely Simulated Pearl**

THEN CONTINUE
LUCKY STREAK W
SWEETHEART OF

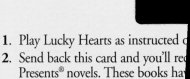

1. Play Lucky Hearts as instructed

2. Send back this card and you'll rec
   Presents® novels. These books ha
   each, but they are yours to keep

3. There's no catch. You're under n
   We charge nothing — ZERO —
   And you don't have to make any
   purchases — not even one!

4. The fact is thousands of readers
   from the Harlequin Reader Ser
   of home delivery…they like get
   BEFORE they're available in st
   prices!

5. We hope that after receiving yo
   remain a subscriber. But the ch
   or cancel, anytime at all! So wl
   invitation, with no risk of any

Ross gave a dry bark of laughter. 'Well, it's certainly better than being stuck in a South American jungle! Incidentally, you were quite right,' he added with a grin, raising himself up on his elbow as he turned to face her. 'That mine *was* an absolute dump. Surrounded by stagnant water—not to mention rampant yellow fever amongst the natives. I don't reckon either of us would have lasted very long. So, it's probably just as well that you *didn't* come with me, isn't it?'

'Yes, I suppose so…' she muttered, wrapping her thin arms about her knees as he watched the waves beating on the sandy shore.

'You "suppose so"…?'

Flora shrugged. 'There's not much point in us hacking over the past. But there's no point in not being honest with one another either. I…well, I've had a lot of time to think since my accident,' she told him quietly, continuing to avoid his gaze as she stared blindly out to sea. 'And I've come to see that our marriage never really stood a chance. We were both far too young and foolish to sustain a serious, adult relationship.'

'I won't argue with that diagnosis,' he agreed dryly. 'But what have you been doing during the past few years? And what's this about an accident?'

'It wasn't the end of the world—although I certainly thought so at the time.' She gave another shrug of her slim shoulders, before explaining how it had affected her career. 'Still, it could have been a whole lot worse. I was lucky to end up with nothing worse than curly hair and a scar at the top of my forehead.'

'Let me see,' he said, raising a hand to catch hold of her upper arm.

'There's nothing worth seeing,' she protested, trying to shake off his grip.

'Don't be such an idiot, Flora.' He laughed, pulling her swiftly down towards him. Taking no notice of her cry of protest as she found herself suddenly lying on her back, he quickly brushed the curly hair back from her forehead.

'Satisfied?' she enquired grimly as he stared down at the long, thin white scar on her hairline.

'Hmm…your surgeon seems to have done a great job.'

'Yes, he did,' she snapped. 'Now, if you've *quite* finished having a good look at his handiwork…'

'There's no need to act like an outraged virgin,' he grinned. 'I have, after all, seen a good deal more of you in the past!'

'That isn't…that's definitely *not* something I want to remember,' she muttered nervously, only too well aware of the tanned face filling her vision and the hard strength of the long, muscular body now lying so close to her on the soft sand.

'You may not want to remember…but I'm quite sure that you do,' he murmured, his hand moving gently down over her face to the soft hollow at the base of her throat. 'Just as I haven't forgotten—despite our being parted from one another for so many years.'

'Cut it out, Ross!' she croaked, swallowing hard and desperately trying to ignore the feather-light touch of his fingers, now trailing slowly over her shoulders and gently brushing aside the narrow straps of her bikini.

But he didn't seem to be listening, his hand continuing its unrelenting path towards the soft swell of her breasts, his fingertips gently tracing delicate, sensual patterns over her quivering flesh.

'Please! This is madness…crazy…completely insane…' she grasped, unable to prevent herself from trembling beneath his touch.

'I may well be out of my mind. But quite frankly, Flora,

I simply don't care,' he told her firmly in a low, husky voice as he deftly untied the bow at the front of her bikini. 'You're still my wife—and I want to make love to you. Nothing else seems to matter a damn.'

His words seemed to be echoing hypnotically in her brain as she stared helplessly up into the glittering blue eyes staring fixedly down into her own.

Yes, she *was* still technically his wife, of course. But…but letting him make love to her would be, without doubt, an act of total folly. When Ross had walked out, it had taken her a long, long time to get over his desertion. Have you forgotten all those lonely nights, weeping into your pillow? she screamed silently at her weak, foolish self. Why make a fool of yourself yet again? Especially as you *know* that his idea of 'making love', is merely a euphemism for having sex. So, come on—pull yourself together. Tell him to get lost!

But she couldn't. Not when her body was now throbbing with a long denied, overwhelming need for his touch. And, despite the certainty of knowing with every fibre of her being that she would live to bitterly regret her decision, Flora determinedly banished from her mind any thoughts of future unhappiness. It was only the here and now that seemed to have any relevance; her whole existence was encompassed by the fierce, savagely driving force of sexual passion and desire.

Abandoning herself to her fate, she trembled as wild spasms of nervous excitement race through her veins at the touch of his warm hands caressing her naked breasts, the fingers moving erotically over her hard, swollen nipples causing her to give an involuntary gasp of sheer pleasure.

'You're so beautiful…so desirable,' he breathed thickly. 'When we were in the water, it seemed as if I was watching an enchanting pale sea nymph, drifting elegantly amongst the coral strands. A strange, beguiling creature from another world, another planet. One in which—'

'For heaven's sake, Ross!'

'Hmm...?'

'You may be a successful author,' she told him, with a breathless gasp of almost hysterical laughter. 'But...but would you mind *not* writing the book? Not just at the moment? Maybe later...?' she whispered, lifting her arms and winding her fingers through his thick dark hair.

'Later...' he agreed huskily, smiling down at her for a moment before rolling over to trap her body beneath his long, lithe figure, crushing her bare breasts against the thick mat of dark curly hair on his chest. 'Much...much later!' he whispered as he firmly possessed her quivering lips, kissing her with a sensual, erotic hunger which left her scarcely able to catch her breath.

Revelling in the hard strength of the arms clasping her so tightly, she could feel the pounding beat of his heart against her own, and the hard, muscular strength of his own sexual arousal. And then, as his mouth left hers to press light, butterfly kisses down the long line of her neck and on over the burgeoning fullness of her breasts, a deep throbbing in the pit of her stomach suddenly flared into harsh, pulsating shock waves of thrilling excitement and his lips closed over the swollen rosy tips, taut and aching for his touch.

With her body on fire and her senses reeling out of control at the soft, seductive warmth of his tongue brushing rhythmically against her nipples, she could only writhe with helpless abandon beneath him.

It had been years since they'd made love together, and her need of him was so desperately intense that she barely noticed when he roughly tore away both her bikini bottom and his own brief pair of swimming trunks. She was only aware of his wide, powerful shoulders blotting out the sun and the powerful heat of his strong body, whose rippling muscles tensed beneath the soft, sweeping touch of her hands.

A savage growl broke from his throat as she raked her nails down his backbone. Deep shudders vibrated through his tall frame and their mutual desire suddenly burst into flames, a scorching, burning heat which swiftly devoured them both as their bodies merged in the frenzied, unleashed hunger of their overpowering need of one another.

Totally uninhibited, their lovemaking was wild and barbaric. Just as a snake would slough off a skin, so their outward images of beautiful, icy-cool model and handsome, sardonic author were totally discarded as they rekindled the deep, raging storm of passion and desire which had first brought them together all those years ago.

Flying higher and higher, it seemed as though they were no longer two separate entities but were welded into one being as they climaxed together, before free-falling slowly back down to earth.

It was some time before either of them moved. Totally exhausted, Flora felt as though she were back once again amongst the coral reef, floating mindlessly on a current over which she had no control yet which still held her securely within its grip.

It was Ross who eventually broke the companionable silence. Carefully untangling their entwined limbs, he pressed a soft kiss on her forehead before rolling over onto his back and staring up at the blue sky.

'Well, well...!'

It was strange, Flora thought sleepily, that with just that one short, repeated word he could manage to convey so many emotions: surprise, considerable satisfaction and... and undertones of something else, which she couldn't quite define. She was still trying to solve the puzzle when the silence was disturbed by the rhythmic drone of an engine, which seemed to grow louder with each passing minute.

'Oh—*hell*!' Ross groaned, quickly sitting up and shielding his eyes from the sun as he stared up at the sky.

'Come on—hurry up! I've got to get back,' he continued, jumping to his feet and quickly putting on his blue shirt and white shorts before packing away the snorkels and coffee Thermos in his canvas bag.

'It's only an aeroplane. Why all the panic?' she murmured, smiling with contentment as she yawned and stretched her languorous body.

'Because it will be arriving at the landing strip in a few minutes—that's why,' he told her tersely.

She turned her head to grin up at him. 'Big deal!'

'Don't be irritating, Flora,' he grated impatiently, quickly jerking away the tartan rug.

'Hey! What on earth do you think you're doing?' she cried, stunned at finding herself suddenly tipped onto the fine, powdery white sand. 'So a plane is landing here on the island. So what?'

'So...I have to be there to meet it.'

It was the oddly constrained note in his voice which, together with the sight of her usually cool, sophisticated husband now looking distinctly perturbed and highly uncomfortable, immediately put her on the alert.

'What's so important about that plane? Why do *you* have to be at the landing strip?' she demanded, scrambling to her feet and brushing the fine sand from her naked body before searching for the two small pieces of her bikini, which seemed to have disappeared without trace.

However, when he remained silent, apparently preoccupied with rolling up the tartan rug, she suddenly realised exactly *who* must be on the plane.

'Oh, my God—it's your girlfriend, isn't it? That film star, Lois something-or-other?'

'I didn't say that,' he retorted quickly.

'No—you didn't,' she agreed grimly. 'Because even someone with *your* brass nerve might find it hard to confess just how quickly it's "off with the old and on with the new",' she ground out furiously.

'You've got it all wrong. The fact is, Lois and I...well, we're not exactly what you might call an item. She and I...'

'What do you mean "not exactly an item"?' Flora turned on him in fury. 'Either she's your girlfriend or she isn't. Right?'

'Well, yes. But...'

'You...you slimy *toad*!' she hissed. 'All that sweet-talk, that lovemaking, just a few minutes ago—it meant *nothing* to you. It...it was just a set-up, right? Especially since you must have *known* your girlfriend would be flying in any minute. So, what were you trying to prove?' she cried, feeling totally sick and ashamed of herself for being such a fool. 'Was it some kind of crazy revenge? Well—congratulations, Ross. Because if you intended to make me look a silly, totally pathetic, foolish woman you did a really *great* job!'

Ross raised his hands. 'Now, Flora—keep calm! There's no need to jump to hasty conclusions,' he muttered as she gave a loud bellow of rage.

'I'm perfectly calm!' she ground out through clenched teeth as she abandoned the hunt for her bikini, angrily scrambling into her pale blue shorts and T-shirt. 'Can you deny that it's your girlfriend in that plane? Or that you invited her to join you on this island?'

'No, I can't deny either of those charges,' he admitted with a shrug. 'But if you'll just give me a chance I can explain everything. The truth is—'

'I don't want to hear any of your damn explanations! And, don't talk to me about "the truth". Because you don't know the meaning of the word—*you dirty rat!*' she yelled, trembling with fury as she grabbed hold of the long cords of the canvas bag. Swinging the bag wildly around in the air, she screamed with laughter at the sound of a satisfactory 'thump' as she landed a direct hit on the side of his dark head.

'*Ouch!*'

'Serves you right!'

'What in the hell did you do that for, you stupid girl?' he growled angrily, wincing as he raised a hand to his face.

She gave a harsh peal of laughter. 'Oh, dear! Poor old Ross. It looks as if you're going to have a black eye, doesn't it?'

'Yes, it damn well does.' He grimaced with pain.

'Never mind,' she told him in a vicious, saccharin-sweet tone of voice. 'Who knows? You might get lucky. Maybe Lois what's-her-name goes for men with really nasty-looking purple and green bruises on their faces?'

'You really are a first-class bitch, aren't you?'

'That's rich coming from you, of all people!' She gave another peal of shrill, angry laughter. 'Because you're clearly nothing but a…a randy two-timing, conniving *bastard!*'

There was a long, heavy silence as they glared fiercely at each other, before Flora turned abruptly on her heel, walking quickly and determinedly back to the Land Rover.

Having successfully managed to deeply insult one another, they conducted their journey back to her cottage in an icy, frigid silence which was only broken as Ross brought the vehicle to a halt.

'Now, see here, Flora...' He sighed. ''We've got to have a long, serious talk.'

'Nuts to you!' she snarled, quickly jumping down and slamming the passenger door shut. 'Goodness knows, I should have divorced you years ago. However, just as soon as I can get hold of a phone, I'm ringing my lawyer and telling him to get rid of my foul, double-dealing, rotten husband—as soon as possible!'

'Go right ahead—that's just fine by me!' Ross retorted savagely. 'In fact, I can't wait to get rid of such a stupid, bad-tempered and totally unreasonable wife,' he ground out through clenched teeth, before slamming the vehicle into gear and roaring off in a cloud of dust.

CHAPTER SIX

'YOU'RE doing fine, darling. Now, look back over your shoulder. Raise your left arm slightly higher…hold it…that's great.'

Doing her best to ignore the crick in her neck and the aching muscles in her outstretched arm, Flora gazed back up at the palm trees behind her as Keith Tucker quickly checked his light meter before moving in closer for a head shot.

'OK. Relax everyone. We'll take a break for ten minutes,' he said a few moments later, handing the camera to his assistant as the make-up girl, Sarah, hurried over to dab the perspiration from Flora's brow.

'Keith's terrific, isn't he? So cool and calm, with none of the usual fuss and drama,' Sarah murmured, carefully touching up the green eyeshadow on the other girl's eyelids. 'I tell you—it's a real privilege to be assisting such a famous photographer. He definitely makes most of the other guys I've worked with look like bumbling amateurs.'

'Yes, he's one of the best,' Flora agreed, grateful for the opportunity to shake the stiffness out of her arms and legs as Keith and his assistant, Jamie, set up the next shot.

In fact, while her private life seemed to have hit an all-time low, she had to admit that camera-wise the past two days had been a great success.

True to his promise, Keith had managed to keep Bernie

well away from all the photographic sessions. 'What's the point of employing a dog and then trying to bark yourself?' he'd asked the other man bluntly, before giving virtually the same message to both Claudia and Helen.

As a consequence of Keith's firm stance, which had resulted in an untroubled and hassle-free working relationship between all the professionals concerned, it looked as if they were well ahead of schedule.

A fact now confirmed by Georgie as she trudged across the hot sand carrying a cool-box containing an assortment of cold drinks.

'I hear we've only got a few more days' filming to go,' she told the two girls, handing Flora some icy-cold mineral water. 'Isn't it sad? I wish we could stay here for ever. Lazing around the pool at the Plantation House and—'

'Get a grip on life, Georgie!' Sarah cried, seizing hold of the bottle just as Flora was raising it to her parched lips. 'How many times do I have to remind you about using straws?' she sighed impatiently. 'Are you trying to undo all my good work or what?'

'Oops! Sorry, Sarah. I forgot.' The plump girl gave her a slightly ashamed grin, quickly placing a straw in the bottle before carrying the cool-box over to the photographer and his assistant.

'Sharing a cottage with that dopey creature is driving me right up the wall,' Sarah muttered, waiting while Flora satisfied her thirst before applying a fresh coat of gloss to the model's lips.

'Georgie can't seem to turn around in a room without breaking something. I've been dropping heavy hints along the lines that she might like to share someone else's cottage.' She looked hopefully at Flora. 'I don't suppose that you...?'

'No way!' Flora quickly retorted with a snort of grim laughter. 'Quite apart from anything else, I wouldn't be able to stand the constant stream of mindless gossip.'

'Tell me about it!' The make-up girl gave a heavy sigh as she put away her brushes. 'I reckon I'll go bananas if I have to listen to any more nonsense about who's doing what to whom in Hollywood,' she added with a rueful laugh, teasing the other girl's blonde curls into a more windswept look.

'Although I have to admit that the stupid girl is right about one thing at least,' Sarah continued. 'This really *is* a lovely island. I can't help wishing we could stay here a lot longer—don't you?'

No, I don't! Flora thought grimly as she forced herself to give the other girl a bright, false smile of agreement. Because as far as she was concerned she'd never hated a place so much—or been so desperately unhappy—in her entire life.

Despite doing her best to avoid Ross like the plague, the past two days had been a total nightmare.

After the spectacular row which had followed so quickly on the heels of their lovemaking on the beach, Flora had been almost incandescent with rage. Determined to contact her lawyer as soon as possible, her fury had increased by leaps and bounds when she discovered that, despite the internal phone system on the island, there was only one line to the outside world. And that—surprise, surprise!—appeared to be firmly under lock and key in Ross's study.

'I'm sorry, Mizz Johnson, but the boss has given orders that it can only be used on his say-so,' she had been informed by his housekeeper, Sophie. A jolly, warm-hearted-sounding woman, she'd been very sympathetic when Flora had stressed the importance of her call to London.

'I'd sure like to help you,' Sophie had sighed regretfully. 'But Ah'm afraid you'll have to sort it out with Mr Ross.'

With an almighty effort, Flora had managed to hold onto her temper as she apologised for wasting the housekeeper's time before putting down the phone in her cottage and swearing out loud with anger and frustration. Grinding her teeth with rage, she'd paced up and down the sitting room, trying to work out what to do next.

It was, of course, just possible that Ross might allow her to use his phone—but she wouldn't bank on it. It was far more likely that the swine would take a considerable delight in being as difficult as possible. Ever since she'd landed on this horrible island he'd done everything he could to upset her. And that humiliating session on the beach earlier in the day had been the final straw.

How *could* he? How could he be so...so... Words had failed her and she'd waved her arms helplessly in the air, desperately wishing that she could blot the whole ghastly episode from her memory.

What on earth had possessed her? Why...oh, *why* hadn't she been sensible earlier that morning? Why hadn't she taken heed of her basic, instinctive knowledge that to allow Ross to make love to her would be an act of total folly?

Because she was a pathetically weak, blithering idiot—that was why! she'd screamed silently at herself, before staggering into the bedroom and throwing herself down onto the soft mattress in a storm of bitter tears.

Mentally and physically exhausted, Flora had clung to the safe privacy of her cottage for the rest of the day. According to Georgie, who'd popped her head around the door to deliver the latest gossip about Lois Shelton's arrival, it seemed that just about everyone else had been suffering from the effects of the previous night's party.

'Most people have opted to eat in their own rooms,' she told Flora, who was attempting to hide her swollen red eyes behind a large pair of dark glasses. 'Shall I ask them to deliver your supper here, to the cottage?'

'Yes, please,' Flora murmured, grateful for an excuse to avoid the rest of the party. 'I'm still not feeling too good, and so...'

'You're not the only one!' Georgie laughed. 'Even poor Ross is wearing a *huge* pair of sunglasses. The word is that he's really trying to hide a black eye, although no one seems to know how he got it.'

'Maybe you should ask his girlfriend?' Flora muttered grimly.

'Who...?' Georgie gazed at her in startled amazement for a moment, before giving a shriek of laughter. 'Don't be ridiculous, Flora! Everyone *knows* that Lois and Ross are crazy about each other. In fact,' the plump girl added with a giggle as she made her way to the door, 'I shouldn't be at all surprised if they aren't making mad, passionate love right this minute!'

Which only goes to show, that those who make nasty remarks get their just deserts, Flora acknowledged dismally, racked by pangs of green jealousy as Georgie closed the door behind her. Even the news that Ross was now sporting a black eye did little to alleviate her feelings of misery and deep unhappiness.

It was at some point in the early hours of the next morning when Flora woke from a restless, disturbed sleep to find her face and pillow wet with tears. As she lay staring up into the darkness of the hot night, she realised that she'd been aroused by the sound of her own desperate sobbing. Try as she might, she couldn't recall ever shedding such unhappy, helpless tears—not since her life, and her heart, had been shattered by Ross when he'd walked out on their marriage all those years ago.

However, when she awoke the next morning, to find the early-morning sun seeping through the lattice shutters of her bedroom, she did her best to try and pull herself together.

Irrespective of her private misery and unhappiness, Flora knew that she had no choice but to fulfil her contract. And that despite her fervent wish to be thousands of miles away—from both her husband and this awful island—she must just grit her teeth and complete the job she'd been hired to do as fast as possible.

Much would depend upon the speed at which Keith worked, of course. But the famous photographer was well-known for not wasting either his or the client's time. So with any luck she would only have to stagger through a few more days before escaping back to London.

Gazing in the mirror, and talking sternly to herself as she smoothed concealing make-up over the dark shadows beneath her eyes, Flora tried to concentrate on bringing cold, hard, rational common sense to bear on the situation.

There was no point in trying to fool herself. Because it was as plain as the nose on her face that she'd been behaving like a perfect idiot. In fact, right from the first moment she had set foot on this island, she'd done nothing but make one damn-fool mistake after another.

So...OK...it wasn't exactly the end of the world, Flora reassured herself quickly. Even allowing herself to be seduced by Ross's overwhelming attraction—and falling a willing victim to the deeply buried emotions which had so completely engulfed her mind and body—could be explained as merely a bad case of *déjà vu*. It was, after all, a well-known fact that a woman never forgot her first lover. So maybe it wasn't all that surprising that she'd temporarily lost her head?

However, there was nothing to be gained from looking back. Or in castigating herself for past mistakes. The important thing now was to concentrate on putting as much distance as possible between herself and Ross. Unfortunately this was a tiny island, and it wouldn't be easy to avoid her rotten husband and his girlfriend, Lois Shelton. But she would only have to hack it for a short while. Stay cool, stay calm...and stay out of trouble, was going to be her motto for the next few days. And then—hopefully!—she'd be rid of both this place and Ross for ever.

After giving herself such good, sensible advice—and bracing herself to face a tough scenario—Flora felt oddly confused and taken aback to discover that the 'lovebirds' had flown, having apparently decided to spend some time on Ross's boat, sailing around the neighbouring islands. However, she'd been so preoccupied by the problems involving herself and her husband, she'd forgotten all about her employer.

When not actually in front of the camera, Flora had hoped that she might be able to remain within the safe seclusion of her small cottage. After all, she *did* have to stay well out of the sun, so that her skin remained the same colour for the photographs. So, she'd assumed—wrongly, as it turned out—that no one would think it odd or peculiar if she didn't mix with the other members of the camera crew around the pool at the Plantation House.

Unfortunately, Bernie Schwartz was not used to being thwarted. After an extremely loud, massive loss of temper, he finally accepted Keith Tucker's stern injunctions to keep well away from Flora and the camera crew when they were working. But he made it clear that he expected Flora to be by his side at all other times.

'Just remember that I'm paying you a helluva lot of money,' he announced with a wide smile which wasn't reflected in his calculating, cold grey eyes. 'And you do want to keep Uncle Bernie happy—right?'

Flora was sorely tempted to tell 'Uncle Bernie' to take a running jump off the nearest cliff. But she managed to hold her tongue, merely contenting herself with giving him a brief, smiling nod of agreement. However, it didn't take a very high IQ to realise that she was going to need help and support if she wished to avoid the obnoxious man. Which was why she forced herself to pay a visit to Claudia and Helen's pink cottage early the next morning.

After knocking nervously on the door, Flora did her best to alert the older women to the awkward, difficult problem she was facing with their employer. All to no avail.

'I don't understand what you're talking about,' the older woman drawled, not even bothering to look up as she concentrated on painting her nails a particularly re-volting shade of blood-red. 'Mr Schwartz is a well-known and highly respected businessman.'

'I *know* he's the boss,' she told the other two women impatiently. 'But I was hired as a photographic model—there's nothing in my contract that says I'm expected to "entertain" the loathsome man. Right?'

'Really, Flora! There's no need for such a crude re-mark,' Claudia grated sternly. 'I'm quite sure he has no intention of being anything other than kind and friendly.'

'Oh, yeah? Well, it all depends on how you define the words "kind and friendly", doesn't it? I mean...' she turned to Helen '...how would *you* like to have his hot, fat, clammy hands wandering all over *your* body?'

'Well, yes…I do see that…' Helen's voice trailed nervously away as Claudia glared at her. 'On the other hand…'

'There's no "other hand"—because the two he's already got are quite bad enough!' Flora flashed back angrily as she strode towards the door. 'And it's no good either of you trying to put pressure on me to keep quiet about this. Because if you don't tell dear old Uncle Bernie to behave himself *I'm* going to be the one to cancel the contract!' she announced grimly, before slamming the door loudly behind her.

It had, of course, been a calculated bluff, since Flora was only too well aware that as far as her contract was concerned she hadn't really got a leg to stand on. Not if Claudia ever found out about her marriage to Ross.

I won't think about him—*I won't*! she told herself now, desperately trying to rid her brain of both her husband and what he and his girlfriend were likely to be doing on that boat of his, miles away from any prying eyes.

But the thought of the famous film star—whom she'd yet to meet—the recollection of the other girl's beautiful face and fabulous figure, refused to be banished from her mind. If only Bernie Schwartz—instead of pestering the life out of her—could have taken a shine to Lois Shelton. A famous film star must have plenty of experience in coping with besotted fans—and therefore wouldn't have any problem in making mincemeat of the awful man.

Concentrating on standing motionless as Sarah carefully adjusted the gossamer-thin pale green and white lengths of chiffon artfully draped over her slim body, Flora indulged in a delicious fantasy in which her employer was well and truly cut down to size. But it was no good wasting her time in futile daydreams, she reminded herself regretfully. In real life, alas, people very rarely got their just deserts.

And then, as if like a bolt from the blue, she suddenly realised that Bernie—like herself—hadn't yet set eyes on Lois Shelton. So, what if...?

With her mind racing at what seemed to be the speed of light, Flora almost shrieked out loud with hysterical laughter.

Yes! That would definitely be the answer to almost all her problems. Because there was no way that Bernie would continue to be interested in her own slim form and pale colouring—not when compared to the American film star's beautiful face, flamboyant red hair and, above all, her sexy, curvaceous figure.

So...all she had to do, Flora told herself excitedly, was to stay well away from the Plantation House until Bernie had an opportunity to take a good, hard look at his host's girlfriend—preferably in a skimpy bathing-suit. And the rest, as they say, would be history!

However, as far as she was concerned, the best...the *very* best thing of all...was that Ross would be absolutely furious! Not that Bernie was likely to be much of a long-term threat to her husband, of course. But, having already experienced her employer's blindly optimistic, bull-headed approach towards any woman he fancied, Flora had no doubt that Bernie was quite capable of causing Ross the maximum amount of trouble.

'Come along, darling. Playtime's over!' Keith Tucker's voice suddenly broke into her thoughts, bringing Flora abruptly back to earth with a bump. 'I've just got one more reel of film to go and then we'll call it a day. So, let's get this show on the road!'

With the light fading fast, Flora concentrated firmly on the work in hand, and it wasn't until Keith and Jamie were busy packing up their camera equipment that she gave any thought of how to avoid the entertainment planned for this evening.

'I'm really looking forward to the barbecue,' Georgie announced as Sarah began removing Flora's make-up. 'What's more, I hear that Ross has arranged for some limbo dancers to give us a demonstration on how it's done.'

'That sounds fun,' Sarah agreed. 'Although I don't think much of your chances of squeezing beneath a low bamboo pole. Not unless you lose some of that weight.'

'Who cares?' Georgie gave her a good-natured grin. 'The food here is far too delicious for me to face going on a diet. And, in any case, my money's on Flora. She's slim enough to slip through a keyhole.'

'Oh, no...I really don't think it's my sort of thing,' Flora muttered quickly. 'I was planning to have a quiet night, and...'

'Why do you always have to be such a party-pooper?' Georgie cried. 'Quite honestly, from the way you've been clinging like grim death to that cottage of yours anyone would think that you didn't want to mix with the rest of us.'

'That's a really stupid remark,' Flora snapped, suddenly realising that this nosy, inquisitive girl was becoming potentially dangerous. At this rate, unless she managed to put her off the scent, it wouldn't be long before Georgie would find out exactly why she was trying to avoid any contact with Ross.

'Or maybe you're trying to be deliberately offensive?' she continued sternly. 'Because, if so, I'm quite happy for us to discuss this matter further, with Claudia Davidson.'

Watching the blood draining from Georgie's face at the mere threat of being dragged in front of 'Cruella De Vil',

Flora couldn't help feeling a pang of conscience. But, while she was sorry to be so hard on her, it was definitely about time that Georgie learned to mind her own damn business.

'I'm sure she didn't mean anything. Just being her normal stupid self,' Sarah interjected quickly, before grabbing hold of the plump girl's arm and dragging her away across the sand.

Flora wasn't able to hear what the make-up girl was saying to Georgie, but from the way that Sarah was waving her hands furiously in the air it looked as if she was not only tearing her off a strip for making such a stupid remark, but also taking the opportunity to release some of her own anger and frustration with her room-mate.

Unfortunately, Flora knew that having created such a fuss she was going to have to put in an appearance at the Plantation House tonight. But when Keith announced that after all their hard work today they deserved to cool off with a dip in the pool, it seemed like a good idea. Maybe putting in an appearance now would allow her to slip away much earlier in the evening?

Unfortunately, it turned out to be a thoroughly rotten idea.

Any plan she might have had—such as enjoying a quiet swim before relaxing on a lounger beneath the shade of a palm tree—was blown sky-high by Claudia and Helen. As soon as she laid eyes on the two older women, looking irritated and bored to death as they sipped long, icy-cool pina coladas by the pool, she feared the worst. And how right she was!

After making a great fuss over Keith—Claudia being nobody's fool and knowing the project would be nothing without his genius with a camera—the two women completely ignored Flora as they proceeded not only to talk

about their absent host and his girlfriend but to speculate
about the character of Ross's first wife.

'I really think the poor woman must have been out of
her mind,' Helen said with a sad shake of her head.

'Very possibly,' Claudia agreed, spreading more oil
over her leathery skin. 'But then, some women are simply
too stupid to know when they're well off. What do you
think, Keith?'

He shrugged. 'Who knows? Maybe they were both just
too young and impetuous,' he told them, clearly not interested in pursuing the subject as he turned and dived
into the pool.

Helen frowned. 'I still don't understand. I mean…if *I*
was married to such a gorgeous man, you wouldn't catch
me leaving him on his own for five minutes—let alone
whole evenings at a stretch!'

'You're so right, dear.' Claudia nodded. 'I would never
have made such a mistake with my own dear, late husband,' she added, with a fond glance down at the large
diamond ring on her hand. 'I always say that the biggest
thing in a man's trousers should be his wallet.'

Helen responded to this pronouncement with a syco-
phantic ripple of laughter.

'Oh, Claudia—you're *so* amusing!' she trilled, before
belatedly realising, as her companion turned to glare at
her, that the other woman had been speaking in deadly
earnest. 'I mean…um…what I meant to say was that
you're absolutely right.'

'Of course I am,' Claudia snapped. 'Being a successful
career woman is all very well. But there's no denying the
fact that the most useful labour-saving device is still a
husband with money.'

Careful not to make another mistake, Helen frantically
nodded her head in agreement, before returning to the

subject like a dog worrying at a bone. 'I still don't understand why anyone would want to abandon a man who's both terrifically attractive and very, *very* rich.'

'Why, indeed?' Claudia shrugged her bony shoulders. 'The woman was clearly an idiot. On the other hand, I have it on good authority that she was a raving nymphomaniac.'

'Good heavens!' Helen gasped, her cheeks flushed with excitement. 'How *simply* awful. Poor Ross!'

Flora seethed with impotent fury at being forced to listen to this quite outrageous malicious nonsense.

Although light years away from being a nymphomaniac, she would have died rather than confess the very uncool truth: that Ross had been her first and virtually only lover. There had also been a stupid one-night stand with a complete stranger, which had happened soon after Ross had left her. That disastrous episode—which had been prompted more by sheer loneliness than any real desire—had left her feeling not only heartily ashamed of herself but also determined never to make the same mistake again.

She hadn't, of course, ruled out the possibility that she might eventually fall in love again, with a man whom she could both love and respect, but until that happened she'd been quite content to concentrate on her work and rely on one or two regular escorts, who were happy to take her out on the clear understanding that a dinner invitation didn't include her bed as a last course.

Which made it not only infuriating, but positively sickmaking to find herself forced to listen to those two foulmouthed women talking such rubbish. How would *they* like to sit by listening to their characters being torn to shreds? And why should they be interested in Ross's ex-wife, anyway? Especially since he now had a glamorous new girlfriend—Lois Shelton.

However, despite having been given the cold shoulder by Keith, the nasty old battle-axes had now found a perfect audience in Georgie. Sarah, of course, had far more sense. After listening to the ridiculous nonsense for a moment or two, she'd wandered away and was now enjoying a swim in the pool. However, that silly girl, Georgie, was clearly in seventh heaven, having the time of her life as she lapped up every scurrilous word about 'poor Ross' and the 'awful cross' he'd had to bear for so many years.

Suddenly deciding that she couldn't bear to listen to any more insane drivel, Flora quickly rose from her lounger and dived into the water. Venting her fury by ploughing up and down the pool in a fast crawl, she eventually slowed down, only to discover that the group had now been joined by their host, his girlfriend and Bernie Schwartz.

Treading water from her vantage spot in the deep end, Flora was in a perfect position to see that her plans regarding the marketing director of ACE had been absolutely spot on. In fact—not to put too fine a point on it—dear old 'Uncle Bernie' was looking totally gobsmacked!

With his tongue hanging out, and almost panting like a thirsty dog, her employer was gazing at the scantily dressed film star as if he'd just been presented with an early Christmas present.

And who could blame him? As she stared mesmerised at the gorgeous figure of Ross's girlfriend Flora suddenly found herself almost gasping with pain, frantically clutching a bar at the side of the pool to stop herself from slipping down into the depths of the water in an agony of depression.

Even from this distance there was no mistaking the fact

that she was looking at real, genuine beauty and a charismatic charm which had already produced a dramatic effect on the group of people by the pool; even Claudia's normally haughty, sour-looking face was now glowing with a happy smile.

The girl's deeply tanned hour-glass figure, barely covered in a minuscule pink bikini, left virtually nothing to the imagination. With a fiery mane of shoulder-length wavy hair surrounding a perfect heart-shaped face, enormously wide blue eyes and a mouth which curved as sensually as her firm, full breasts, Lois Shelton could only be described as 'drop-dead gorgeous'. *No wonder* Bernie's eyes were practically bulging out of their sockets!

And no wonder that her husband had quickly dumped her, before rushing off to meet this girl's plane, Flora told herself glumly. It would have taken far more self-control than Ross possessed to resist the allure of every red-blooded man's dream come true. In fact, she hadn't a moment's hesitation in acknowledging that Lois Shelton was, quite simply, the most beautiful and sexy woman she'd ever seen.

'I'm just wondering whether to slit my throat now or wait until later,' Sarah murmured wryly as she swam up to join Flora. 'Goodness knows, I've done the hair and make-up of some really lovely women in my time—but I've *never* seen anyone to beat that gorgeous creature!'

'I've just come to exactly the same conclusion,' Flora agreed with a heavy sigh. 'Only, in my case, I was contemplating jumping off the nearest cliff.'

'Oh, come on! You're a fantastic-looking woman, who'd normally knock spots off anyone,' Sarah told her firmly. 'It's just that...'

'It's just that we're both looking at sheer perfection,'

Flora acknowledged with another deep, heavy sigh. 'In fact, to be entirely honest, I have to say that compared to that stunning bird of paradise I appear to be merely a dusty sparrow.'

Since there was no disputing the truth of Flora's statement, they both lapsed into a depressed silence, neither of them able to tear their eyes away from the vision on the other side of the pool.

'Ah, well...' Sarah sighed. 'Maybe she's a total bimbo and as thick as two short planks?'

Recalling her husband's short fuse, and his irritation in the past with any woman, however beautiful, whom he'd thought of as either stupid or silly, Flora reluctantly shook her head. 'No, unfortunately I've got a gut feeling that she's probably as smart as paint.'

'If so, it looks as if the fairy godmothers were *definitely* working overtime at her christening.' The other girl grinned before announcing that it was time she left the pool to get changed for the evening's barbecue.

Slowly following Sarah down to the shallow end, Flora realised that she simply wasn't in a fit state to handle any sort of meeting, however brief, with either Ross or his girlfriend. Which meant that the only way of avoiding the lovers was to slip away into the Plantation House and hope to find a downstairs cloakroom in which to shower and change, before quietly making her way back to her cottage.

Unfortunately, while she easily managed to achieve her first objective, once she'd made her way inside the house Flora found herself becoming confused by its sheer size. Anxious not to bump into any servants, who might well wonder why a dripping wet woman was padding down their immaculately cleaned corridors, she furtively turned the handle of one door after another, without success.

Her heart thumping with rising panic, almost whimpering with fright at the likelihood of being discovered any minute, Flora peered carefully around a bend in the corridor. A moment later she gasped with relief as she saw an arched opening through which could be glimpsed a luxurious bath and shower complex.

Moving swiftly across the marble floor, she had almost reached the bathroom when she was abruptly halted in her tracks by the sound of a deep voice.

'Just where in the hell do you think you're going?'

Oh, no! This couldn't be happening to her—it simply *couldn't*!

'Well...?' Ross demanded as she spun around, her face white with shock at being discovered by her husband—who seemed to have just materialised from thin air, like an evil genie.

'I...er...I was just looking for... I wanted to...'

'Could it be that you were looking for my study?' Ross drawled sardonically. 'Yes, my housekeeper, Sophie, did tell me that you were *very* anxious to make a phone call to London,' he added with a hateful grin as a deep crimson flush swept over her pale face. 'But I see no reason why I should pay for an expensive international call to your lawyer. So, you'll just have to wait until you've left this island, won't you?'

'You...you miserable skinflint!' she hissed furiously. 'And I *wasn't* looking for your rotten study. I...well, I merely wanted to take a shower. But only if you can afford to let me use some of your hot water, of course,' she added sarcastically.

Ross gave a snort of grim laughter. 'Yes, I reckon I can just about stand the cost of that item. In fact, it sounds like a great idea.'

Quickly striding forward, he gripped hold of her arm,

not pausing in his momentum as he swiftly frog-marched her into the large bathroom.

'Ouch! That hurt,' she grumbled, rubbing her arm as she turned to see him closing and bolting the door behind him.

Staring blankly up at his tall figure, it was some moments before Flora could cudgel her brain into some kind of working order. All she could seem to think about was how outstandingly attractive and sexy he was looking in his dark navy thin cotton polo shirt over a pair of brief navy shorts, his long, lean brown legs ending in a pair of dark blue sneakers. And it wasn't until he began taking off his shoes that her confused mind finally started to get its act together.

'What…what *on earth* do you think you're doing?'

'Well, it was your idea.' Ross shrugged as he bent down to undo the laces.

'My idea…?' Flora echoed blankly, closing her glazed eyes for a moment and banging a fist hard against her curly head in an effort to unscramble the jagged pieces of her brain. '*What* idea?'

He gave a heavy, impatient sigh. 'You suggested having a shower. Now, since I've been out on the boat all day—'

'Are you out of your tiny mind, or what?' she shouted. 'I…I wouldn't have a shower with you…you *slimeball*—not for all the tea in China!'

'And as you're looking thoroughly hot and bothered it seems like an excellent idea,' he continued, ignoring both the furiously angry words and rigid figure of his wife, as he proceeded to strip off his shirt.

'I'm certainly *not* "hot and bothered",' she raged. 'And if you aren't out of here in five seconds flat, I'm going to scream blue murder.'

'And let everyone know that you're having a shower with your husband...? I don't think so.' He grinned, moving determinedly towards her.

'Leave me alone!' she ground out, backing quickly away across the shiny marble floor. 'I'm so fed up with my awful contract that I don't care *who* knows about our marriage. And...and besides,' she added quickly as he came nearer, 'I know you wouldn't want Lois to find out that you're really a foul, two-faced, double-dealing *rat*!'

He gave a low, sexy laugh. 'Lois is a big girl. Believe me, she's perfectly capable of looking after herself.'

'Go away!' She gasped as her backbone came into cold, sharp contact with the marble wall. 'It's been a hell of day, and I...I simply can't take any more of this nonsense...'

And then, to her utter consternation and the complete astonishment of both herself and Ross, she suddenly burst into a storm of tears.

'For God's sake, Flora!' he ground out, moving swiftly to catch hold of her slim figure as her knees buckled beneath her and she began sliding slowly down the wall. 'I've never known you to cry like this. What on earth's got into you?'

'I don't know,' she wailed, a heavy lump in her throat as she leaned helplessly against him, her falling tears caught like dew drops on the short, curly dark hair of his hard, bare chest.

'Calm down—everything's going to be all right,' he murmured softly, his arms closing gently around her trembling figure.

'No. No, it isn't,' she sobbed, knowing that she was all kinds of an idiot but simply not able to stop herself from savouring the forbidden warmth and security of his tall, strong figure.

A moment later he was gently lifting her face up towards him and carefully blotting the tears from her eyes with a nearby hand-towel. His tanned, handsome face was so close to her own that she could feel his breath caressing her cheek, and then he lowered his head a fraction, softly pressing his lips to her damp eyelids and on down over her pale cheek, the touch of his mouth brushing across her trembling lips almost beguiling in its gentleness.

Desperately trying to ignore the devastating effect he was having on her mind and body, she seemed temporarily helpless against the insidious, hot, pulsing wave of desire and excitement suddenly scorching through her quivering figure. And then, with a final massive effort of will, she managed to wriggle out of his embrace.

'I'm sorry I...I behaved so foolishly just now.' She sniffed, before doing her best to draw an invisible mantle of dignity about herself as she straightened her weary figure and looked him directly in the eye.

'It's been a long day and I expect that I'm just tired, that's all. However,' she added as he opened his mouth to speak, 'I have no intention of having a shower with you. As far as I'm concerned, our marriage is dead and buried. And, despite behaving like a stupid teenager a few days ago, I have no wish or desire to make such a mistake *ever* again.'

'Oh, come on, Flora—we both know very well that it was no "mistake",' he told her roughly. 'Surely you must have realised, as I did, that we're two halves of the same whole. That whatever errors we've made in the past there's no reason why we can't make the effort to try again.'

'Good sex is one thing—life and love are quite another,' she told him grimly. 'Not only did you leave me once—but you're more than likely to do it again. And, while honesty might compel me to admit, after seeing Lois Shelton, that I can well understand why she's utterly irresistible, I'm damned if I'll play second fiddle in that particular orchestra!'

'How can you be such an idiot?' he growled. 'Lois and I are good friends, of course, but—'

Flora gave a shrill laugh. 'Pull the other leg, Ross— and give me credit for having *some* intelligence! But, in any case,' she added grimly, 'I don't care how "friendly" you both are. The plain fact is that I'm *never* going to forgive you for rushing off to see her, only moments after making love to me.'

'And that's your final word?' he ground out through clenched teeth.

'You're damn right it is!' she retorted bitterly, quickly seizing up a large, long-handled back-scrubbing brush and brandishing it menacingly in his face.

Ross stood staring intently down at her for a moment, before giving a heavy sigh and shaking his dark head as he turned and walked slowly towards the door.

'You've accused me of not respecting your intelligence, Flora,' he told her with a grim bark of sardonic laughter. 'But even that remarkably stupid girl, Georgie, appears to have more sense in her little finger than in the whole of that empty brain of yours!'

CHAPTER SEVEN

DESPITE the heat, Flora couldn't seem to stop herself shivering with nerves and tension as the noise of the bathroom door, slammed viciously hard by Ross's departing figure, still seemed to echo around the marble-lined room.

Standing beneath the warm needle-spray of the shower, and determinedly scrubbing every square inch of her skin—as if by doing so she could cleanse away all trace of Ross from both her mind and body—proved to be completely useless. Because, of course, there was no point in trying to fool herself any longer.

Deep in her heart, she now saw that she must have always known the truth. Right from the moment she'd first landed on this island—even when she and Ross had fenced, snarled and fought so bitterly with each other—she'd struggled against acknowledging the fact that she still cared deeply for her husband. Mainly, of course, because getting involved once again with Ross could only be a recipe for disaster.

Flora could still recall the sage advice from one of her older friends: 'Never trust a man who's dumped you once—because he'll do it again and again and again.' Her husband's behaviour, since she'd landed on this island, had merely underlined the truth of her friend's words.

However, Ross was quite right—you really *are* a dribbling idiot! she told herself roughly as she turned off the shower. Even thinking how she'd almost succumbed to his overwhelming attraction a few moments ago was enough to make her skin crawl with shame and embarrassment.

Surely she ought to know by now that a sensual, vibrantly masculine man like Ross would be used to seizing what he wanted. Just as for a brief span of time, the other morning on the beach, he'd happened to want her. However, their lovemaking had clearly meant little to him other than satisfying a temporary appetite. Because as soon as the plane carrying Lois Shelton had flown over the island he'd quickly dumped Flora in the trash can, before hurrying off to sample yet another, more exotic dish.

So, why should she still feel anything for such a man? A man who was, quite clearly, nothing more than a double-dealing, amoral, two-faced *swine*?

'I hate him…I really *hate* him!' she ground out through clenched teeth, furiously rubbing herself dry with one of the huge, fleecy white bath towels piled high in this luxurious bathroom. I hope his next book bombs completely, that a hurricane destroys everything on this horrid island and that luscious Lois takes to comfort eating and ends up weighing *at least* sixteen stone, she told herself viciously, before sinking down onto a stool as the weak, feeble tears began flowing down her cheeks once again.

What's the use of fighting against fate? she thought, leaning her weary head against the cool marble wall for a few moments, before grabbing some tissues to blow her nose. You've always loved the rotten man. And—since you're such a blind, stupid fool—it looks as if you always will.

Not able to face the prospect of seeing Ross again, so soon after their confrontation, Flora waited until everyone had gone off to change and the coast was clear before slipping away from the Plantation House.

She was sorry to miss the barbecue, and the opportunity of witnessing the local limbo dancers. However, the fact that she was hungry, and her stomach was rumbling, was a small price to pay—especially when compared to the quiet and solitude to be found in her own small cottage. Besides, when rushing from one couturier's show to another during the Paris Collections, for instance, there were many times when her only sustenance had been black coffee and the occasional croissant. So, it wouldn't hurt her to go without a meal. Not if it meant avoiding having to see Ross and Lois entwined together, Claudia and Helen being bitchy, and Bernie being Bernie.

However, whether it was because her stomach was rumbling, or the fact that her mind was in turmoil, Flora barely had a blink of sleep all night. Tossing and turning through the long, stifling hot dark hours of the night, she eventually gave up the unequal struggle and rose at first light, deciding on the spur of the moment to go for a walk by the sea shore.

It took her much longer than she'd imagined to find a way down to the beach. But maybe that was her own fault, since she'd been determined to keep well away from the Plantation House.

However, a large grove of banana and mango trees had provided a superlative breakfast, and, by the time she found herself approaching the pale cream, talcum powder-like texture of the sand edging the ocean, Flora was feeling a whole lot better for both the exercise and the fresh air.

She blithely slipped off her sandals, and it was only when she straightened up that she discovered she wasn't alone. Even though he was standing with his back to her, she had no problem in recognising the tall, dark-haired figure clothed in a singlet and shorts, engaged in close conversation with another man beside a rocky outcrop at the side of the beach.

Feeling sick, and frozen into immobility by a sudden rush of blind panic, she looked wildly about her for somewhere to hide. But there was nothing other than a small group of tall, brilliantly coloured Flamboyant trees on the other side of the beach. With no obvious shelter nearby, Flora realised with a sinking heart that she had absolutely no hope of avoiding another confrontation with Ross.

She could, of course, swiftly turn tail and run away. But even as the thought entered her head her husband's companion glanced in her direction and gave her a friendly wave.

'Hello—you're up bright and early,' Keith Tucker called out, before bending down over a rock pool to retrieve a small object which he handed to Ross.

With no possibility of avoiding the two men, Flora realised that she was just going to have to cope with the situation as best she could. But at least she wouldn't have to face her husband on her own. With any luck the presence of Keith would prevent Ross from being either too rude or aggressive.

Taking a deep breath, she forced herself to walk slowly across the sand, her bare feet squelching through the pools of sea water left behind by the ebbing tide. 'What are you two doing here at this time of day?' she queried, marvelling that she was managing to sound so calm and relaxed, when in reality her stomach was churning like a food mixer on fast forward.

'My wife is mad on shells, and she made me promise to bring some back home with me,' Keith said, bending down to carry on washing the sand from what looked like a small pink conch.

Ross, who hadn't moved since she'd hailed the two men, now turned slowly around to face her.

If looks could kill...! she thought hysterically, unable to prevent herself from taking a quick step back, flinching as she saw his lips curl in distaste, his hard, stormy blue eyes raking her figure in a swift glance of what appeared to be pure, unadulterated loathing.

'Hello, Ross,' she muttered, staring fixedly down at her bare feet. Struggling to overcome a stupidly childish impulse to burst into tears, she was staggered to hear herself adding inanely, 'It's...um...it's a lovely day.'

'That's what I thought—until a few moments ago,' he drawled, his voice icy-cold as he regarded the bowed head of the girl standing in front of him. 'However, the sight of you probably won't spoil Keith's day.'

The implication being that she'd definitely spoilt his? Thanks a bunch—*you rat*! she railed at him silently, her nails biting into the palms of her clenched hands. She wouldn't...she would *not* give him the satisfaction of losing her temper in front of the photographer. But it was proving difficult to control herself. Especially since, even though she was determinedly avoiding his gaze, she could feel the heat of his scorchingly angry eyes practically burning holes in her sleeveless pale blue lawn blouse, hanging loose over a pair of tight denim shorts.

'Keith tells me that there's only one more day's work to go. So, it seems as if you'll be flying back to London very soon. I expect you're looking forward to that, hmm?'

She shrugged. The tears were very near the surface now, and if her voice broke or wobbled she was lost. Raising her head and taking a deep breath, Flora forced herself to look him straight in the eye. 'Yes, I am looking forward to going home. The sooner the better. Lounging around on an island, however beautiful, is *not* how I'd like to spend my life.'

Thank goodness for Keith! she thought hysterically as Ross regarded her with cold fury, his tall frame shuddering for a moment before he brought his rage under control.

A moment later he was turning to Keith and giving the other man a friendly slap on the back. 'I expect I'll see you later at the Plantation House,' he said, pointedly ignoring his wife as he jogged down the beach.

Her legs feeling like jelly, Flora leaned for support against a nearby rock, staring helplessly after the fit, lithe figure now swiftly disappearing into the distance.

With a heavy sigh, Flora made a supreme effort to pull herself together. She had, after all, made her feelings very plain to Ross yesterday. So she couldn't really expect him to treat her with anything but acute dislike. All the same, there was no need for him to be quite so...

'Are you interested in shells?'

'Hmm...?' She looked blankly at the photographer. 'I'm sorry, Keith, I didn't hear what you said. The thing is, I...um...I haven't quite got my act together this morning,' she added lamely.

'None of us are feeling too bright,' he agreed with a wry chuckle. 'I was just wondering if you're a collector, too?'

'Well, no. But, it certainly seems as if you've been busy,' she murmured, gazing at the large canvas bag on a rock beside him, containing all kinds and sizes of empty shells. 'I don't know anything about them, but I must say this certainly looks very different,' she added, picking up one shaped like a round vase.

'Ah, yes—*globivasum*. It was discovered by Abbott in

1950, I think. Now, that really *has* made my day,' he told her enthusiastically. 'It's only found in Antigua and the Lesser Antilles, you know.'

Despite her general gloom, Flora couldn't help laughing. 'No, I *didn't* know that fascinating piece of information. Nor did I realise that you had such an unusual hobby. And don't try and pretend that this is just your wife's pastime,' she teased. 'Because anyone who can quote the Latin name for that thing has to be a mad enthusiast!'

Keith gave her a slightly shamefaced grin. 'Yes...I'll admit that we're both keen shellers. But please don't tell anyone,' he added hastily. 'People are apt to think it very childish.'

'Your secret is safe with me,' Flora assured him. 'Besides, some of these are really very beautiful.' She picked up a large shell, admiring its delicate, iridescent soft pink colour, which gleamed and sparkled in the early-morning sunshine.

Encouraged by her appreciation, Keith showed her some of the places where the best shells were likely to be found, before offering her a hot mug of coffee from a Thermos he'd brought with him.

'Mum...this is wonderful,' Flora murmured, perched on a flat rock as she sipped the hot liquid, savouring the view of large sea birds silently wheeling and diving over the ocean. 'I wish life could always be like this...so amazingly quiet and peaceful.'

'It certainly makes a change from last night!' Keith agreed dryly. 'What did you think of the limbo dancers?'

'I wasn't there,' she told him, before adding hurriedly, 'I was feeling rather tired, and...and decided to have an early night.'

'A very sensible decision, as it turned out. I imagine that there will be quite a few sore heads, this morning.'

Flora turned to look at him. 'A case of the dreaded rum punch strikes again?'

'Well...' He hesitated. 'I think everyone probably had too much to drink—which didn't help matters, of course. But, I'm afraid Bernie Schwartz was mainly to blame for the fracas.'

'Come on, Keith,' she demanded impatiently as he fell silent for a moment. 'Tell all!'

He laughed. 'You're as bad as Georgie.'

'Hardly!' she grinned. 'But, what's all this about a "fracas"...?'

'Hmm...well, it seems that our employer has apparently fallen hook, line and sinker for our latest visitor.'

'Lois Shelton?'

He nodded. 'You can't blame the man, of course. Because she is, without doubt, quite spectacularly beautiful. Unfortunately Bernie made no secret of the fact that he was suddenly head over heels in lust, and was clearly making a perfect nuisance of himself. Which wouldn't have been a major problem,' Keith added reflectively. 'Not if Lois had been allowed to cope with him on her own. Because she struck me as very street-smart—and more than capable of handling the Bernie Schwartzes of this world.'

'So, what happened?'

Keith shrugged. 'I was pouring myself a drink at the time, and so didn't see too much of the action. However, it seems that Ross—who, I must say, had been in a simply foul mood all night—suddenly grabbed hold of Bernie and chucked him in the pool.'

'Well done Ross!' Flora exclaimed, forgetting for a moment just how much she hated her rotten husband.

'My sentiments exactly,' Keith agreed with a grin. 'Unfortunately, Bernie landed in the deep end and promptly sank like a stone. Even more unfortunately, it was one or two moments before everyone realised that the stupid man had never learned to swim.'

'Oh, Lord!'

Keith nodded. 'Yes, it could have all ended in disaster. And if it had been left to Claudia and co, who were running around the edge of the pool, squawking like chickens who've just had their heads cut off, it probably would have. Quite honestly, Flora, the scene was like something out of Dante's *Inferno*. Everyone yelling and shouting fit to burst in the semi-darkness, and most of them far too drunk to do anything constructive except scream at the top of their voices.

'Anyway, I heard Ross, who hadn't been drinking, call out to Lois to switch on all the outside lights before quickly diving in to the deep end. And a moment later he was hauling Bernie out of the pool—apparently none the worse for his unexpected swimming lessons!'

'Goodness knows, I can't *stand* Bernie,' Flora admitted with a slight grimace. 'But, it was a really stupid thing for Ross to do. Especially as it could so easily have ended in tragedy.'

Keith nodded. 'You're quite right, of course. However, our employer wasn't at all fazed at his near escape from a watery grave—which, in all honesty, I have to say he'd partly dug himself. In fact, after spitting out some water, Bernie merely yelled for another glass of rum punch before agreeing to let Ross drive him back to his cottage. In fact,' Keith added with a shrug, 'like or loathe the man—you have to admit that Bernie is one tough *hombre*.'

'Yes, well...I hope it's taught Ross a lesson not to lose

his temper in future,' Flora snapped, the violent mood swings which seemed to be affecting her lately now causing her to feel furiously angry with her husband. 'But, since he always was such an obstinate pig, I don't suppose he'll mend his ways. I don't know how many times I used to have to tell him to calm down, and…and…'

Her voice trailed slowly away as she suddenly noticed the photographer's raised eyebrows, and the fact that he was now regarding her with wry amusement.

'I mean…I've always heard that he…I don't actually know him that well, of course…' she babbled incoherently, desperately trying to recall exactly what she'd been saying a moment ago.

'Relax, Flora!' Keith smiled. 'It's been perfectly obvious—to me, at least—that you've had some sort of relationship with Ross in the past. But these things happen all the time. It's hardly the end of the world, right?'

'It looks like it's going to be the end of *my* world,' she exclaimed helplessly, blinking rapidly as her eyes suddenly filled with tears. 'If you've guessed the truth, it's only going to be a matter of time before Claudia and the rest of them find out. In fact, I'm amazed that Georgie hasn't already broadcast the news far and wide.'

'Hey, calm down,' Keith told her firmly. 'So, you and Ross have had a love affair in the past—so what?'

'It wasn't just a love affair—he's my *husband*!' she wailed, raising a hand to dash the stupid tears from her tried, weary eyes. 'I always meant to get a divorce but somehow never got round to it—mostly because I was always so busy. And now there's the business of the contract, you see, and…and…if everyone learns the truth, I'm going to be up the c-creek without a p-paddle.'

'Whoa!' Keith gazed at the unhappy girl with grave concern. Flora had always appeared to be so strong and confident. It was quite a shock to see her now, weeping her heart out as she sat beside him, her tall, slim figure hunched in bleak misery. 'Why don't you tell Uncle Keith all about your problems? It will do you good to get it off your chest.'

'It will certainly make a change from dealing with dear old "Uncle Bernie",' she muttered, giving him a wobbly smile as she gratefully accepted the handkerchief he was holding out to her. And, by the time she'd finished explaining all the complicated ramifications which had resulted from her stupid action in signing that damn contract, Flora had to admit that she did feel a lot better.

'I've been an idiot, haven't I?' she sighed heavily.

'Well...maybe "not too bright" would be a better description,' he agreed with a warm smile. 'However, as I said, it's certainly not the end of the world. Because I'm quite sure that no one else in the company has any idea that there was a past relationship with Ross—let alone the fact that you're married to him.'

'But if you guessed then surely it won't be long before they come to the same conclusion?'

Keith shook his head. 'I doubt it. For one thing, it's my job to look behind the face of a model. Searching for and attempting to show various aspects of the inner personality is what makes a good picture. And don't forget,' he added, 'I've photographed you many times in the past. So, not only did I realise, fairly early on, that you had something major preying on your mind, but once I started looking I soon picked up the vibes between yourself and Ross.'

'The only vibes between us are mostly composed of a mutual, acute dislike of one another,' she told him grimly.

He shrugged. 'All I know is that the air is positively

electric whenever you're in the same room together. Are you *quite* certain that it's all over between you and Ross?'

'I thought you'd taken a good look at Lois Shelton?' Flora retorted caustically. 'Since she's his latest girlfriend, I don't think there's much point in even bothering to answer that question, do you?'

'Probably not,' he agreed sadly, and turned his attention to pouring them both another cup of coffee.

'Tell me, Keith,' she said after a while, 'what's the *real* secret of a happy marriage? I've often wondered if there's some hidden, magical ingredient, known only to a few lucky people?'

He shook his head. 'It's no good asking me—because I haven't a clue. Even though I've been happily wed for twenty-five years, I still wouldn't pretend to know why some marriages work and others don't.'

Which was a fat lot of help, she thought dispiritedly as he glanced at his watch and announced that it was time he got on with some work. 'I've arranged to do some pure location shots, this morning,' he added, packing up his canvas bag. 'So, I won't need you until later this afternoon.'

Some time later, walking slowly back to her cottage through groves of waving palm trees, Flora heard the sound of an approaching engine. Glancing back over her shoulder, her heart gave a sickening lurch as she recognised Ross's Land Rover. Quickly bracing herself to expect the worst, she was startled to see that the person in the driving seat wasn't her husband, but his girlfriend.

'Hi!' Lois called out as she slammed on the brakes, bringing the vehicle to a sharp, sudden halt amidst a cloud of dust.

'I don't think we've met.' Lois leaned over the side of the Land Rover, regarding Flora with a broad, friendly smile. 'I'm just staying with Ross for a few days. It's a great island, isn't it? Really cool. Are you part of that crazy ACE team? I sure hope not,' she laughed. 'Oh, boy! Are they a bunch of weirdos—or what?'

Feeling somewhat dazed at the rapid-fire, conversational style of this spectacularly beautiful girl, Flora admitted that, unfortunately, she was indeed modelling for the cosmetic company. 'Although you're quite right,' she added, unable to prevent herself from smiling back at the other girl's infectious grin. 'Most of them are definitely very strange indeed.'

'Ah! A woman after my own heart. Where are you going?' Lois asked, not waiting for the answer as she bent over to open the passenger door. 'Jump in.'

'No, really...there's no need to bother,' Flora told her quickly. 'I'm just going back to my cottage, over there.' She turned to point to the small building, half hidden amongst the trees in the distance.

'Oh, great! I've been *dying* to see inside one of those pretty little houses. How about if I offer to trade a lift, in exchange for a cold drink and a good snoop around your cottage?'

Later, as she carried two glasses out onto the small veranda, Flora was still wondering what on earth had possessed her to give in so easily. Admittedly it had soon become clear that when Lois had set her heart on something she was a hard act to deal with. Talk about being steamrollered!

However, despite not wanting to get involved in any way with someone who was currently dating her husband, Flora couldn't help liking the girl. In fact, leaving aside her outstanding good looks and terrific figure, Lois appeared to be a thoroughly nice and amusing girl. She certainly didn't seem to have any of the usual affectations, or the pampered, spoilt attitude to life normally associated with Hollywood film stars.

'I hope this doesn't contain any alcohol?' Lois said as she took the glass from Flora's hand.

'No, it's just pure orange juice.'

'Like almost everyone else, I seem to have drunk far too much last night.' Lois gave her a rueful grin. 'Have you come across the rum punch they serve here on this island? Believe me, kid, it's real *dynamite!*'

'I know what you mean,' Flora nodded sympathetically. 'We all felt really ill following a party on the day we arrived. Which is why I've more or less been on the wagon ever since.'

'A good move,' Lois agreed. 'It's a pity some of your companions didn't learn the same lesson. Because after last night I imagine a lot of them are definitely enjoying Hangover Hotel this morning!'

Flora grinned. 'Yes, I've heard all about my employer's unexpected swimming lesson.'

'That Bernie Schwartz—what a scumbag!' Lois exclaimed wrathfully. 'He came on to me like a heat-seeking missile, for heaven's sake. Not that I couldn't have handled the slimeball with one hand tied behind my back,' she added quickly. 'In my line of work, those sort of guys are an occupational hazard. Which is why it was so stupid of Ross to get involved.'

'It was an extremely silly thing to do,' Flora agreed. 'Especially since Bernie could have so easily drowned. And, while I personally can't stand the man, even *he* doesn't deserve that sort of dreadful fate.'

Lois shuddered. 'I can't even bear to think about it. I was simply *furious* with Ross, who'd been in a thoroughly nasty mood all night. And I still don't know what had upset him.' She shrugged, brushing a hand through the waves of her fiery red hair. 'I mean, we'd had a lot of fun sailing around in his boat. And he was perfectly all right when we returned to the Plantation House. Then, for some unknown reason, he began prowling around, snapping and snarling at everyone, like a reincarnation of Attila the Hun.'

Not quite knowing what to say at this point, Flora went back inside the cottage to fetch some more orange juice. Opening a carton and pouring the contents into a jug, she quickly tried to think how to handle this awkward situation.

She had no quarrel with the young film star, who clearly knew nothing about the relationship between herself and Ross. Indeed, under any other circumstances she'd have enjoyed meeting Lois and they might have become good friends.

However, she *really* didn't want to get into any discussion about her husband. Especially as it must have been their confrontation in the shower room, late yesterday afternoon, which had led to his display of bad temper. Although why *he* should have been going around like a bear with a sore head, she had no idea. Surely if anyone was entitled to be thoroughly upset by what had happened it was definitely *her*? Right?

However, having spent a sleepless night going over and over that scene in her mind, there was nothing to be gained in thinking about it now, Flora told herself firmly. So, maybe her best course of action would be to plead tiredness or a heavy work schedule—and get rid of Lois as quickly as possible?

Unfortunately, despite giving herself such good advice, Flora found it practically impossible to put it into action. Because no sooner had she returned to the veranda than

Lois almost gave her a heart attack by asking, 'I was just wondering how long you've known Ross?'

'Er…well…I only arrived here on the island a few days ago,' Flora muttered evasively, trying to control her trembling hands as she carefully placed the jug on a small table.

Luckily Lois didn't seem to have noticed that she hadn't directly answered the question. 'He's a terrific writer. Have you read any of his books?'

'No…no, I haven't. Although everyone says they're very good,' Flora added quickly.

'The screenplay he wrote for my last film was absolutely brilliant! So, I guess it's mostly due to Ross that we all won so many Oscars,' the other girl told her with a happy laugh. 'When my agent first told me about it, I wasn't too sure about accepting the part. And then, after reading the script, even I could see that it was bound to be a winner.'

And so are you, Flora thought silently, unable to fault the other girl's fresh, clear complexion, or her voluptuous figure beneath a pair of skin-tight white shorts topped by a skimpy, low-cut white T-shirt—which looked as if it had shrunk *at least* two sizes in the wash. As Lois placed her hands behind her head and leaned back in the chair, causing the twin peaks of her magnificent breasts almost to burst through the thin material, Flora could only feel deeply, *deeply* depressed.

'Of course, I'd never met Ross before we started work on the film,' Lois told her with a happy smile. 'In the beginning I was totally wrapped up in learning my part, costume fittings and all that usual stuff, but then we found ourselves on location together and I suddenly discovered that he was a really terrific guy.'

'Yes, well, I really do have to get ready for work, so…'

'For instance, he seemed to have endless patience—rewriting parts of the script for the male lead, Phil Guest. Phil can be a real pain in the neck—especially if he thinks he isn't getting enough good lines. But Ross handled him brilliantly.'

As Lois continued to blithely expand on the virtues of Ross Flora realised that the other girl was totally wrapped up in her new romance and simply not capable of thinking about anything else. So, there seemed nothing she could do or say, at the moment, other than tough it out—and wait until Lois ran out of steam.

'I'm crazy about the guy, of course. Which is why it's such a drag that he's being so stubborn and refusing to get a divorce.'

'*What?*'

'Oh, yeah.' Lois turned to look at the blonde girl who was gazing at her with startled eyes. 'Didn't you know that Ross was married?'

'Well, I...'

'Apparently he got hitched years ago. He and his wife—some ritzy model—are separated, and haven't seen each other for a long time. All this happened well before he became a famous author, of course,' Lois explained. 'And so, although Ross won't discuss the problem, I reckon that must be the reason why he doesn't want to get a divorce. What do you think?'

'I...I'm afraid I really don't know what to think,' Flora muttered helplessly, not having any idea of what the other girl was talking about.

There seemed no rational reason why—when this fantastic-looking girl was clearly so mad about him—Ross was apparently refusing to get a divorce. And, in any case, he knew very well that she was going to see her lawyer in London as soon as possible. So, what Lois was saying simply didn't make sense.

'Are you quite sure...?' Flora hesitated for a moment, feeling decidedly guilty about discussing her husband's intentions with his current girlfriend. It was low, sneaky and thoroughly deceitful behaviour on her part, and she knew that she ought to be utterly ashamed of herself.

'It sounds as if you must have made a mistake,' she continued, defiantly ignoring a sharp pang of conscience from her better self. 'I can't imagine that Ross would want to remain married, especially to a wife he hasn't seen for a long time. Not when he could have an amazingly beautiful girl like you.'

'Well, that's nice of you to say so.' Lois grinned, before giving a slight shrug of her shoulders. 'But you also spend your life in front of the camera. So you know that being born a good-looking gal is only a kind of useful tool as far as your profession is concerned. It's got nothing to do with the person you are inside, right?'

Flora nodded. 'You're absolutely right. I just wish that everyone else could get the message.'

'You and me both,' Lois agreed gloomily. 'I mean, it's no secret that I've made all the running as far as Ross is concerned. I really thought that giving him hardly any warning and just turning up here on the island might do the trick. To show him that I don't need hairdressers and beauty parlours, or mind getting my feet wet. But I don't seem to be getting anywhere,' she added with a heavy sigh. 'Maybe having been married to one beautiful wife has put him off trying it a second time. But I reckon it's got a lot more to do with wanting to hold onto the money.'

'The money?' Flora gazed blankly at the other girl. 'What money?'

'Hey—don't be a dope! A famous, successful writer like Ross is worth millions.'

'So...?'

Lois rolled her eyes dramatically up at the veranda roof. 'Oh, wow! Don't tell me you've never heard the word "alimony"?'

'You mean...?'

'Oh, sure. Where I come from it happens all the time. I mean, there's lots of young, struggling actors who get married long before they become stars and hit pay-dirt,' she explained, surprised to have to explain the everyday facts of Hollywood life to this lovely, blonde English girl, who was now staring at her with a stunned expression on her face.

'So, those early marriages often don't survive too well,' she continued patiently. 'Maybe it's his fault, maybe it's hers—who knows? But once the guy in question has made a whole pile of dough he's not too keen to lose it, even if he's busy lusting after someone else. With me so far?'

'Absolutely!' Flora retorted grimly. 'In fact, I think I'm even ahead of you. Because what you're saying is that a wealthy man will do just about *anything* to stop his wife— whom he married when he was poor—from trying to divorce him now that he's rich?'

'Well...I wouldn't have used exactly those words,' Lois said slowly. 'But I guess that's about right. Not that I have any evidence that it's necessarily the case as far as Ross is concerned,' she added quickly. 'He's a really nice, straight guy, who's always been up front and honest with me. It's just...' She gave a shaky, unhappy laugh. 'Well, I guess I may have been stupid and fallen into the trap of believing my own publicity. Which is why I prefer to think that he's turned me down for financial reasons—and not because he just doesn't fancy me or is still in love with his wife.'

'*Rubbish!*' Flora retorted swiftly, suddenly gripped by an overwhelming feeling of strong, female solidarity.

'You are an absolutely stunning-looking girl, with a stupendous figure and a great personality,' she told Lois firmly. 'Anyone who's turned you down or doesn't fancy you clearly needs their head examined. Besides, I can virtually guarantee that Ross *doesn't* love his wife. So, you can bet your bottom dollar that he's trying to hang onto his money. He's nothing but a stingy, money-grubbing *cheapskate*!'

'Wow! I can see that you *really* don't like him!' Lois gave a breathless gurgle of laughter. 'But how do you know that he isn't still keen on his wife?'

Rapidly coming back down to earth, Flora gazed at her wildly for a moment, desperately trying to think of an explanation for her foolish outburst. And then, as her brain remained obstinately blank, she was rescued in the nick of time—by Georgie.

'Hi, Flora—hi, Lois,' she panted, her face brick-red with exertion and her plump figure clearly wilting in the midday heat. 'I've got a message from Keith. He says that he won't need you until tomorrow morning for the final day's work.'

'OK. Thanks for letting me know.'

'Well, I guess it's time I was off.' Lois stood up. 'I'm going back to the Plantation House to cool off with a swim. Do either of you want to come?'

'Oh, yes, please!' Georgie sighed happily.

'How about you, Flora?'

She hesitated for a moment, and then reluctantly shook her head. 'I think I ought to stay here. With only one more day's filming to go, I'd better stay well out of the sun.'

'OK—I'll probably see you later on tonight,' Lois said, leading Georgie towards the Land Rover. 'Thanks for the drink—and the talk!' she called out, before giving a friendly wave and driving off down the path.

It had definitely been a relatively peaceful meal tonight, Flora thought, slowly sipping her coffee out on the terrace and allowing the quiet buzz of various conversations to flow over her head.

But the fact that dinner hadn't been as noisy as usual, might well have been due to the general fright everyone had experienced yesterday, when Bernie had nearly drowned. This had clearly had a sobering effect on the more forceful members of the company. Claudia and Helen, for instance, had been acting in a very subdued manner, while Ross had remained virtually silent the whole evening.

Ross! Even the thought of her foul husband was enough to bring her out in a hot rash. What a rat-fink he'd turned out to be. She glared across the terrace to where Ross was involved in a deep conversation with Keith, the two men ensconced in deep, comfortable wicker chairs.

How she'd managed to remain so calm throughout the rest of the day, let alone keep her cool at supper tonight, Flora had no idea. Because she'd been almost consumed by an overpowering rage, and a determination to teach Ross a lesson he wouldn't forget.

Having simmered down after Lois had left the cottage, she'd done her best to think things through in a calm, rational manner. To be honest, it hadn't been easy to picture Ross in the role of a stingy husband, intent on preventing his discarded wife from getting hold of his money.

Mainly because, when looking back over her brief marriage, she could only recall him being extremely generous. But what had finally tipped the balance and made her as mad as fire was the fact that Ross should now be regarding her as some sort of gold-digger. Well...she'd show him. She'd *definitely* make him wish that he'd never been born!

And, thanks to Lois, she now had the perfect weapon: a divorce! That would teach him to make love to her simply in order to protect her millions. Oh, yes—Mr Moneybags was going to *really* regret two-timing both his wife and his girlfriend.

The thought of Lois prompted her to look around the dimly lit terrace. There seemed no sign of the beautiful girl. In fact, since the end of the meal—at which she and Ross had seemed remarkably unloverlike—Lois seemed to have vanished from the scene.

'Come along, little lady. I'll walk you home.'

Looking up at Bernie's bulky figure as he towered over her chair, Flora gave him a brief smile as she rose slowly to her feet. Her employer was just about the last person she'd want escorting her back to the bungalow. But after her sleepless night she was very tired. And, since he'd apparently transferred his attentions from her to Lois, she shouldn't have any trouble coping with the awful man.

Surprisingly, Bernie seemed none the worse for his ducking. In fact he'd been busy tonight, bullying everyone into spending a few days on Antigua before flying home. Not being particularly interested in sport, watching a pro-am tennis tournament at one of the large hotels wasn't her idea of a good time. But, everyone else—from Claudia to Georgie—had seemed to think it was the best idea since sliced bread.

She waved goodnight to the others and was just following Bernie when a hand snaked out to catch hold of her arm, and she found herself being swung around backwards, hard up against the tall figure of Ross.

'What on earth...?' she gasped breathlessly.

'I don't think it's a good idea to let Bernie walk you home,' he told her firmly. 'If you wait for a moment, I'll get one of the servants to run you back in the Land Rover.'

'Oh, for heaven's sake. You're just paranoid about the man,' she muttered, shaken both by her proximity to his broad-shouldered figure and by the fact that he was looking outrageously handsome in his white tuxedo.

'No,' he retorted curtly. 'It's Bernie who is paranoid about Bernie. Wake up and smell the coffee, Flora,' he added impatiently. 'Even *you* must see that letting yourself be alone in the dark with that man is just asking for trouble.'

'I don't see anything of the sort!' she hissed angrily. 'You're only behaving like a jealous husband because he chatted up your girlfriend. Well...let me tell you that I *have* woken up at last. And I now know *all* about your underhand scheme and *exactly* what you've been planning.'

If Flora had wanted confirmation of everything that Lois had told her earlier in the day, she now knew that it had been nothing but the truth. Because Ross, who'd been regarding her with a cold, glacial expression in his hard blue eyes, suddenly looked startled and extremely guilty—just like a small boy who'd been caught with his hand in the cookie jar.

CHAPTER EIGHT

FLORA had never felt quite so mortified in her whole life. Why...oh, *why* hadn't she listened to Ross?

Her husband might be a thoroughly deceitful rogue, who saw no problem in making love to his wife *and* his girlfriend in the space of a few hours, but at least he was a highly attractive deceitful rogue. While Bernie Schwartz was simply awful and totally *gross*!

So, how could she have been so abysmally foolish as to let Bernie escort her home? Especially since the dreadful man had clearly had one thing—and one thing *only*!—in his rotten mind ever since he'd arrived on Buccaneer Island.

'Now really, Mr Schwartz, you're making a *great* mistake,' she protested, trying to put some distance between herself and Bernie's gorilla-like arms. 'We...we only have a *working* relationship, you know. And my contract certainly doesn't include this sort of nonsense!'

'Who cares about the damn contract?' he demanded huskily, planting his large frame directly in front of her and thus cutting off the escape route to her cottage, only a few yards away. 'It's only a bit of paper. Right?'

'Yes, but it's an important bit of paper,' she retorted quickly, desperately trying to think of a way out of this nasty situation. 'I mean...when I signed it, I promised to stay single and not get involved with any...er...any strange men.'

'Well, I'm def-in-itely no stranger, honey!' he sniggered, before moving closer and grabbing her by the arm. 'And I can tell—a beautiful girl like you needs protection. Am I right—or am I right?'

'You're absolutely, one hundred percent *wrong*!' she panted, vainly trying to push him away. 'I've got all the protection I need, because I...I'm a married woman. I know...I know that I shouldn't have signed the contract, but—'

'That's OK by me, honey—I just *love* married women! They *really* understand a guy's basic needs, if you know what I mean...?' he told her huskily.

'Oh, for heaven's sake! Cut it out—you foul man!' she demanded breathlessly, frantically slapping the huge fat, hairy hands which seemed to be all over her.

'Aw...come on, honey. I've been getting the signals all week. Everyone knows that you're just crazy about old Uncle Bernie!' He leered, trying to get a firm grip on the pesky girl who kept wriggling out of his reach.

'Are you mad?' she cried, kicking him sharply in the shins. 'I wouldn't touch you with a ten-foot pole!'

Bernie grunted with pain at the blow, but it didn't seem to dampen his ardour one little bit.

'Hey—I just love a girl who's frisky!' he growled, finally managing to grab hold of Flora's slim figure and pulling her into his arms once again. 'In fact, I'm just plum crazy about my Botticelli angel! So, whaddya say? Let's get in your cottage and make beautiful music together, huh?'

'*No way!*' she yelled, struggling to get free of this ape in human form. 'Besides, I thought you were supposed to be "crazy" about Lois?'

'Yeah, well...her boyfriend sort of changed my view of things. You know that you've always been *my*

Botticelli angel,' he panted earnestly. 'So, there's no need to be quite so feisty and…*agh*…!' He groaned as she quickly kneed him in the groin.

'There's *every* need!' she yelled, quickly slipping off her shoes and raining blows down on his back and shoulders as he collapsed, doubled up with pain, in the rough grass beside her cottage. 'It's about time you learned to keep your filthy hands to yourself!'

A moment later, the scene was brightly illuminated by the glare of headlamps as a vehicle roared up out of the darkness. Coming to a juddering halt, the driver left the lights on as he leapt out, and a moment later her husband was standing by her side.

Ross's lips twitched as he surveyed the scene in front of him. In the red corner—rolling around on the ground, battered, bruised and moaning for help—was Bernie Schwartz. While, in the blue corner—aggressively brandishing high-heeled, stiletto shoes, her green eyes flashing with rage and looking quite capable of going another ten rounds—stood his wife.

'What took you so long?' she demanded belligerently, still burning with fury and outrage as she scowled menacingly down at Bernie before spinning around to face her husband.

'Well…it certainly looks as if you have the situation well under control,' Ross drawled coolly. 'I don't want to be irritating, but I *did* warn you about letting dear Uncle Bernie walk you home, didn't I?'

'OK—OK! There's no need to rub my nose in the dirt,' she muttered, sweeping the curly hair from her face as she glared up at him.

'Quite right!' Ross agreed with a laugh. 'I rather think that's Uncle Bernie's current position, don't you?'

'Ha…ha!' Flora ground out caustically. 'Incidentally—

just in case you were wondering—you *are* being extremely irritating. So, if you've nothing better to do in the next few minutes,' she added sarcastically, 'I'd appreciate you getting that foul man out of here—*right now!*'

'Bernie clearly isn't going anywhere just at the moment,' Ross told her with a grin, ignoring the man on the ground who was obviously still dazed and confused, begging to be rescued from a woman whom he was now referring to as 'the Angel of Death'.

'So, let's just make sure that you get home safe and sound, hmm?'

'Leave me alone. I'm not a child!' she snarled as he took hold of her arm.

'Of course you're not,' Ross agreed soothingly, helping Flora to put on her shoes before assisting her trembling figure up the wooden steps of the veranda and opening the front door of her cottage. 'You're just feeling a bit shaken, that's all.'

'Yes, well…maybe you're right,' she muttered, leaning gratefully against his tall figure as the anger and fright drained out of her weary body.

'Now, take it easy and drink this,' Ross said, returning from the tiny kitchen with a glass of water in his hand.

She shook her head. 'It's OK. I'll be all right.'

He frowned in concern. 'Are you sure? You're looking a bit pale. Maybe a cup of tea would be a good idea?'

Flora gave a heavy sigh, leaning against the wall and closing her eyes. 'No, I'm fine,' she murmured. 'Besides, it's mostly my own fault for being so stupid. I should have listened to your warning about Bernie.'

'Yes, you most definitely should,' he agreed grimly.

'There you go again,' she grumbled, opening her eyes to glare up at the man standing over her. 'And, if you say "I told you so" once more, I…I'll kill you!'

'Poor old Flora.' He gave a low rumble of laughter. 'It's been quite a night, hasn't it?'

'Yes, it certainly has!' she sighed again, suddenly feeling totally exhausted and bone tired. 'Please just go away and...and leave me alone,' she added in a wobbly voice, ashamed to find herself close to tears.

'I'm not leaving you in this state,' he told her quietly, placing an arm about her trembling figure and walking her slowly into the bedroom. 'Not until I've seen you safely tucked up for the night.'

'Oh...for heaven's sake. I don't need this sort of nonsense.' She sighed wearily as he led her towards the bed. 'I'm a big girl now, and perfectly able to look after myself.'

'Yes, I don't think poor Bernie would quarrel with that statement,' Ross agreed, with a low bark of soft laughter as he swiftly undid the zip of her dress.

'What in the heck do you think you're doing?' she demanded, with her last reserves of strength. 'First Bernie, and...and now you. I need this like...like a hole in the head!'

'Why don't you just shut up?' he asked her sternly, ignoring her weak struggles as he quickly stripped the dress from her slim figure, rapidly following with the removal of her flimsy underwear.

'I hate you! I really, *really* hate you,' she moaned as he whipped back the light cover on the bed before pushing her down on to the mattress and swiftly covering her naked body with a sheet.

'Do you Flora?' he murmured, sitting down on the bed and smiling cynically down into the angry green eyes, swimming with tears. 'I wonder why I don't believe you?' he added, leaning forward to softly brush his mouth over her trembling lips.

'No, Ross…please! I…I can't cope with any of this. Not now. Not tonight,' she begged tearfully. 'Please just go away—and take that awful man with you.'

'As always, your word is my command,' he drawled mockingly, pressing a soft kiss on her forehead before rising to his feet and striding towards the door.

'Hah! I should live so long—you treacherous, two-timing bastard!' she called weakly after him, the sound of his caustic laughter ringing in her ears as he disappeared into the night.

Poised as if in flight, her arms stretched out behind her as she clung to the rigging for dear life, Flora could only be deeply thankful that this was positively the last photo-call. And that in a few hours' time she'd be on a plane to London.

She hadn't been at all enthusiastic when Keith had informed her, at break of dawn this morning, that he wanted to take some final shots of her on Ross's yacht.

Quite apart from anything else, she'd been feeling like death warmed up, and definitely not looking her best. After an exhausting, restless night, during which she seemed to have had little or no sleep, Flora had practically shrieked with dismay on catching sight of herself in her dressing table mirror. In fact, she'd hardly recognised the face gazing back at her, the greeny-white pallor of whose complexion was surmounted by deep shadows beneath weary green eyes.

It had taken a long time before she'd felt able to leave her cottage, having spent what seemed an age in trying to disguise the ravages of the night. Which was why she hadn't exactly cheered at the photographer's sudden change of plan.

'Have a heart, Keith!' she'd moaned in protest. 'You

know that boats are always such a problem, camera-wise. All that bobbing around in the water means that the damn things never keep still. And there's virtually no room to change, or—'

'Calm down—and stop grumbling.' He'd grinned. 'It's only going to be a short session, since everyone's on a tight schedule. And I think that my idea of having you poised on the prow, like a figurehead on one of those old galleons, will provide some stunning pictures.'

Keith had been right, of course. Even though her arms were aching fit to burst as she clutched the ropes behind her, leaning out over the water at an angle of almost forty-five degrees, Flora realised that the famous photographer definitely knew his business.

'Can you lift your head back? And let's have an expression of ecstasy, darling…as if you're rushing to meet your lover,' Keith called out. 'That's great. Just keeping on thinking of dear Uncle Bernie!'

'Ha-ha…very funny!' she said grimly out of the side of her mouth, fed up to the back teeth with having to put up with all the teasing and ribald comments.

Luckily there'd been no sight or sound of Ross. Because she'd quite made up her mind that if he dared to make any reference to what had happened last night— even so much as one brief, small, cynical word—she'd have screamed blue murder.

Not that she'd actually seen Bernie either. Apparently, the foul man had caught the first plane to Antigua earlier this morning. But—wouldn't you know it?—that faithful news-hound, Georgie, had spread far and wide the information that their employer had not only been in a filthy temper, but was also looking thoroughly bruised and battered.

Unfortunately, as far as her future career was con-

cerned, he'd last been seen escorting Flora to her cottage.
So it hadn't taken a genius—let alone everyone else on
the island—to put two and two together. With the result
that not only had she been the heroine of the hour—as far
as the lower echelons of ACE were concerned—but she'd
also had to face a very nasty interview with Claudia Davidson.

As might have been expected—the fierce old dragon
had gone completely ballistic.

During the tirade, which had even had Helen cowering
tearfully in a corner of the room, Claudia had accused
Flora of practically everything under the sun—but mostly
of putting all their jobs at risk. Her charges had also included dereliction of duty, gross misconduct—even Flora,
for all her anger, had been forced to smile at *that*
charge!—and being totally responsible if ACE decided to
abort the Angel Girl campaign.

'As for your contract...' Claudia finally stormed, her
teeth snapping like a hungry crocodile as she carefully
enunciated every word, 'I can tell you, here and now, that
I will be advising Mr Schwartz to cancel it *forthwith*!'

Having stood her ground throughout the whole stream
of invective, Flora merely shrugged her shoulders, safe in
the knowledge that with any luck she held all the winning
cards. Not *quite* all, she quickly warned herself. Because
there was still the vexed question of her marriage to Ross.
However, there was a good chance that 'dear Bernie'
could be persuaded to overlook that little item—especially
if she decided to make life difficult for the slimy rat!

'I quite agree that there's nothing to stop you and Mr
Schwartz from cancelling my contract,' she told Claudia.
'However, I *really* don't think that would be a good idea.
Certainly not as far as you're concerned.'

'Oh, *really*?' the older woman echoed sarcastically.

'Well, I'm not particularly interested in what *you* think, Miss Johnson.'

Flora shrugged. 'Suit yourself, you stupid old bat,' she retorted, grinning as both women gasped with horror and outrage at her temerity. 'But the minute you try to terminate my contract I'll be slamming a law suit on *you*, personally, Ms Davidson.'

'I beg your pardon?' Claudia retorted imperiously. 'I don't think that you quite understand—'

Flora laughed. 'Oh, yes, I do! Believe me, as soon as I've briefed my lawyer in London we'll be taking you to court—probably in America, where they aren't at all keen on hard-working employees being exploited by big business—claiming unreasonable dismissal. Incidentally, I'll also be seeking damages—both for my loss of earnings and the psychological stress you've caused me.'

'What "psychological stress"?' Claudia hissed, almost trembling with rage. 'I've never heard such insolence! Any court would throw such a stupid case straight out of the window!'

'Oh, no—I don't think so,' Flora told her calmly. 'Because I will, at the same time, be taking "dear Uncle Bernie" to court also in the States, claiming that he's guilty of repeated *gross* sexual harassment. And stating the fact that you aided and abetted such harassment.'

'*What?*'

'It's going to be fun, isn't it?' Flora gave her a beaming smile. 'Particularly as I have several witnesses—every one of them highly moral, upright citizens—who will be prepared to back up my evidence in both legal actions,' she continued relentlessly. 'For instance, I shall be calling your friend, Helen, as a witness to the fact that I explicitly reported and warned you about Mr Schwartz's outrageous behaviour. She will be forced to confirm that you took absolutely no notice of anything I said.'

Flora laughed as Claudia turned to glare at Helen, moaning piteously in the corner. 'I don't think she's going to stand up to much cross-examination, do you?' she queried coolly. 'In fact, as I see it, by the time I've finished crying all over the judge and jury, I'm quite confident that they'll award me an absolutely *colossal* amount of money in damages!'

In the stunned silence which followed her words, Flora casually tossed in one or two more grenades.

'And, of course, that still leaves Mr Schwartz—whom I'm also hoping to take to the cleaners financially! Quite honestly, Claudia, by the time I've finished raking in what "dear Uncle Bernie" would undoubtedly call "a whole lotta dough", I fully expect to make at least *double* the amount ACE are paying me. *And* I'll have the satisfaction of knowing that both you and Mr Schwartz will probably have lost your jobs—spending the rest of your days begging for a crust on skid row!'

'You…you can't do this!'' Claudia gasped, falling back in her chair, her face as white as a sheet.

'Oh, yes, I can—and I will!' she retorted grimly. 'If either you or Bernie take even one step out of line I'll have you both in court so fast you won't know what's hit you.

'However…' Flora paused, to allow the brutal facts of life to sink in. '*If* you're sensible, and decide to draw a veil over this unfortunate affair, I'm willing to fulfil my contract. It's up to you,' she added, before turning to march out of Claudia and Helen's cottage. 'Because "quite frankly, my dear, I don't give a damn!"''

Well, there you go. That's probably one more promising career down the tubes, Flora thought wearily now, as Keith called for a short break and a change of costume.

Not that she regretted for one minute having stood up to Bernie and Claudia, she told herself, walking back over the deck, careful not to trip over the coils of rope as she made her way down to the main cabin. Although she wasn't sure whether she'd got that wonderful quote by Clark Gable from the film of *Gone With the Wind* quite right... Still, if it meant the cancellation of her contract, that was just too bad, she thought.

She *could* pursue her threats to sue everyone in sight, of course. But, it was likely to be a 'no win' situation. The cosmetic and perfume industry was riddled with guys who thought models were fair game. And so, even if she won her case, it was more than likely that she'd be unofficially blacklisted—however unfair that might be.

'Ouch!' Flora winced a few minutes later as Sarah helped her out of the long, semi-transparent, sea-green chiffon dress before slipping a classical white silk toga over her head. 'That pose Keith's designed is a real killer,' she added, rubbing the sore muscles in her arms. 'In fact, having to do this session on our last day is nothing but a real drag.'

'Tell me about it,' Sarah muttered, adjusting the gold cords across and under Flora's breasts, before winding them round and around her ribcage, ending in a knot at the back of her slim waist. 'Can you get yourself out of this, if I'm not here?'

'I don't see why not,' Flora assured her. ''What's the problem?'

'The thing is...I really shouldn't leave you in the lurch...' Sarah gave a worried frown. 'But if I don't rush off now, I'll never manage to finish my packing and catch the plane to Antigua.'

'Hey, relax! I'm perfectly capable of managing on my own,' Flora told her, knowing that everyone was on a very tight schedule. With the small landing strip on Buccaneer Island only capable of coping with small, six-seater planes, the company had arranged a shuttle service to ferry everyone over to Antigua.

'Apparently I'm on the last plane with Keith and his assistant, Jamie. Are you going with Claudia, Helen and Georgie?'

'Unfortunately, yes!' Sarah grimaced as she flicked a comb through Flora's hair. 'Still, it is only a short flight, and at least Lois will be good company.'

'But, I thought...?' Flora stared at her in surprise. 'I mean, are you quite sure that Lois isn't staying on the island?' she asked casually, as if the answer was of little interest to her one way or the other.

Sarah shrugged. 'Well, I know Lois was thinking of joining the rest of us in Antigua, for the tennis tournament. But I suppose she may have decided to stay here with Ross. They make a really terrific-looking couple, don't they?'

'Oh, yes—absolutely terrific,' Flora agreed brightly, wishing that she'd kept her mouth shut.

'OK—that's it.' Sarah grinned, careful not to disturb her good work as she gave Flora a hug. 'It's been great fun working with you. Don't forget to give me a ring the next time you're in New York?'

'I won't,' Flora promised. 'And I'll keep my fingers crossed that you don't have to sit next to Georgie on the plane.'

'You and me both!' Sarah laughed as Flora moved carefully up the steps from the main cabin onto the deck.

It's amazing the tricks you can play with photography, she thought, looking down at Keith standing next to the ropes, which were firmly anchoring the boat to the quay-side. By carefully angling the camera he could produce pictures that looked for all the world as if the yacht was gliding smoothly through the rolling waves of an empty ocean.

'You look very Grecian—and very gorgeous!' Keith called up as she once again took up her position on the front rail of the yacht.

'Flattery will get you nowhere.' She grinned down at him. 'Where's Jamie got to? If you've sent him off for more film I'm going on strike!'

'I didn't need the boy, so I sent him off to pack his case. And you don't have to worry—this is positively my last reel,' Keith assured her.

'Wonders will never cease,' she teased.

However, Keith was as good as his word, and in a reasonably short time he'd called it a day.

Arranging that he would wait on deck while she got changed, before accompanying Flora back to her cottage to collect her case, she once again made her way down the steep wooden steps into the main cabin of the yacht.

Five minutes later she plonked herself down on one of the padded bench seats, swearing aloud with annoyance and frustration. What on earth had Sarah done with this flipping knot—tied it with super glue?

After rubbing her arms—which were already aching from taking the force of her weight during the photo session earlier—Flora had another attempt at untying the gold cord, knotted so tightly by Sarah at the back of her waist. But it was no good. The damn thing obstinately refused to budge. Eventually, admitting defeat, she realised that she was going to have to ask for Keith's assistance.

Sighing with exasperation, she rose to her feet. But

she'd hardly taken more than two steps across the cabin towards the companionway when the boat gave a sudden lurch and she found herself falling back down onto the seat once again.

Probably the tide was on the turn. Or maybe it was the swell from another boat coming alongside, she thought, rising to her feet and casting a cursory glance out of the nearest porthole. But there was no other craft visible, just the peaceful scene of light blue sky and deep, greeny-blue sea stretching away in the distance. So it must be the changing tide which was making the boat rock gently back and forth as she made her way across the cabin.

'Keith…? I'm sorry to be a nuisance, but I can't seem to get out of this dress,' she called out as she emerged onto the deck.

However, as she moved past the lowered mast, covered in the shrouds of its neatly bound mainsail, Flora suddenly froze, completely unable to believe the evidence of her own eyes.

OH…MY…GOD!

Almost paralysed with shock, she stared in horror at the deserted quayside, which now lay at least twenty yards away from the boat—the watery gap rapidly increasing with every passing second.

It seemed an age before her numb brain realised the awful truth: someone must have undone the ropes tying the yacht to the quay!

'Keith? *Keith*—where in the hell are you?' she screamed, running panic-stricken around the wooden deck. But the photographer was nowhere to be seen.

Desperately trying to avoid looking back at the quay— now being left well behind as the yacht drifted very slowly out to sea—she concentrated on covering every square inch of the deck. After all, Keith *could* maybe have tripped over some ropes and knocked himself out.

However, after an exhaustive search, she sank down onto a nearby hatch cover, wearily acknowledging that, whatever had happened to Keith, he was no longer on the yacht.

Thinking about it afterwards, Flora realised that it was at this point that she very nearly went to pieces. The reason that she didn't actually run around yelling blue murder, or jump off the boat and try to swim ashore, was simply because she was far too frightened to move even an eyelash—let alone try to stand upright.

Shaking and quivering with fear, she let visions of the yacht suddenly rolling over and sinking without trace, or becoming a modern-day version of the *Mary Celeste*, float through her petrified mind.

After what seemed aeons of time, she eventually began to pull herself together. However, on glancing down at her watch, Flora was astonished to see that it was only a few minutes since she'd discovered her awful predicament. She was still in a dire and extremely dangerous situation, of course. But she was becoming gradually aware that the vessel seemed to be maintaining a steady course.

Gingerly rising to her feet, she noticed that the two small sails in the bow had stopped flapping and were now filling out as the boat appeared to be turning slowly into the wind. Goodness knows how or why, but Ross's yacht seemed—for the moment, at least!—to be perfectly capable of sailing itself.

Thinking about Ross, she felt her eyes fill with tears as she realised she might never see him again. Now, when it was far too late, she would have given everything she owned to feel his strong arms about her. But surely it wouldn't be long before he realised his boat had gone? Maybe even now he was arranging for her to be rescued?

Unfortunately, it was only a few moments later before she realised she was living in a fool's paradise, her heart sinking as she realised that any kind of rescue would be virtually impossible. This yacht was, as far as she knew, the only boat on the island. So, other than being winched up by a passing helicopter, her chances of being saved from a watery grave looked very dim indeed. In fact, barring miracles, the only alternative was to try and sail this vessel back to the island.

Which was *far* easier said than done, Flora told herself glumly. Her only experience of sailing had been confined to messing around with a small dinghy. In fact, what she knew about this sort of huge yacht could be written on the back of a postage stamp.

A few minutes later, desperately trying to keep rising panic at bay, she stood staring blankly at the wheel, which obviously controlled the rudder. Loath to touch it, especially as it appeared to be connected to various wires, which ran up to a funny-looking type of small wind vane at the top of the mast, she decided to go below to the cabin, on the off-chance of finding some sort of sailing manual.

Not feeling at all safe, since she would be trapped if the boat turned turtle, she quickly glanced at the chart-table in a corner of the saloon. But she might as well have been looking at various maps of the moon for all the good it did her. And even discovering that there was a radio transmitter did nothing to improve matters either, because she hadn't the faintest idea how it worked.

Suddenly feeling cold and shivery, despite the heat of the day, she began searching quickly through the two smaller cabins in the stern for something to wear. But, although they were neatly and comfortably fitted out with single bunks, she drew a complete blank.

Further reconnaissance of the layout below deck revealed a small bathroom and a well-fitted galley, whose fridge appeared to contain a surprising amount of food. Also, on opening one of the galley drawers, she found a sharp knife and was—*hallelujah!*—able to cut the cord which had been wound so tightly around her body.

Walking slowly back into the main saloon, Flora was busily employed in unwinding the twisted gold cord from around her ribs when she suddenly heard a faint, indefinable sound. Listening carefully, she realised that it was coming from behind a door, which must lead to a cabin in the front of the boat.

In a blind panic, as she realised that Keith might have fallen through one of the forward hatches and be lying seriously injured, she ran across and wrenched open the door.

Almost fainting in shock, she gazed in sheer disbelief at the sight before her.

Because there, lying on a large double bunk—a paperback book in one hand a half-eaten apple in the other—was her *husband!*

CHAPTER NINE

'WELL...it's certainly taken you long enough to get here,' Ross drawled coolly, taking another noisy, large bite from the apple. 'Not only have I almost finished this extremely boring book but, as you can see, I'm also feeling rather peckish.'

'*P-p-eckish?*' Flora gasped, clinging for dear life to the cabin door as she felt her knees buckle beneath her. Her dazed eyes tried to focus on the tall, rangy figure lying on the bunk. But she couldn't seem to get her act together, her brain still reeling from the shock of suddenly finding Ross, reclining casually at his ease, in the large, airy cabin.

'Of course I'm hungry. It's been a long, boring morning,' he explained in a patient if slightly peevish tone of voice. 'And wondering whether you were likely to do something really stupid—like fiddling with the automatic pilot or wrecking the radio transmitter—didn't do much for my peace of mind either.'

'*Your* peace of mind?' she hissed, trembling violently as a thick red mist seemed to be flooding swiftly through her brain. 'What about the state of *my* mind?

''Now, Flora, if you'll just—'

'Do you have any *idea* of what I've been through during the past half-hour?' she cried, beside herself with fury as she waved her arms distractedly in the air.

'Well, yes. But—'

'I thought Keith had fallen overboard. I thought that the boat would capsize any minute. I thought that I'd be killed and...'

'Darling! For heaven's sake—calm down!' he said, rolling off the bunk and moving quickly to her side.

'Calm down?' she yelled, swiftly whirling away from him and jumping up onto the bunk—the only place in the cabin where he couldn't easily grab hold of her.

'I've *no* intention of calming down,' she screamed. 'I'll kill you! I'll see you hung, drawn and quartered! But first—I'm going to have your guts for garters! Oh, boy— you'll wish you'd never been born. I'll take you to the cleaners in the divorce court. Just *see* if I don't!'

'Yes, I'm sure you'll have a good try,' he murmured, his eyes gleaming with laughter at the sight of his irate wife completely out of control as she stamped furiously up and down on the mattress. 'Whether you succeed is quite another matter.'

'Oh, yeah!' she taunted. 'And just *who's* going to stop me? You...?' She gave a shrill, high-pitched laugh. 'Hah—do me a favour!'

'OK. I've had enough nonsense from you during this past week to last me a lifetime,' he told her impatiently, the amusement dying from his face as he leaned forward and gave her a sharp push which sent her tumbling back down onto the mattress.

There was a long silence as they glared at one another. His blue eyes, beneath their heavy lids, glinted as he stared down at the sprawled figure on the bed—who was now gasping for breath as she angrily brushed the shining, tangled mass of curly blonde hair from her pale face.

'If you think I'm impressed by these caveman tactics— dream on, Casanova!' she jeered breathlessly. 'Macho doesn't prove mucho—certainly not as far as you and "dear old Uncle Bernie" are concerned!'

Ross stared at her, his eyes flashing with fury for a moment. And then, almost unbelievably, she saw his lips curving into a sardonic grin as his broad shoulders began to shake with laughter.

'What's so damn funny?' she demanded wrathfully. 'Believe me, you'll be smiling on the other side of your face when you find all your property seized and your bank accounts frozen. In fact, by the time I've finished with you,' she added with considerable relish, 'you'll be lucky to be left with only the clothes you're wearing.'

Ross laughed. 'That won't worry me,' he drawled, quickly stepping out of the dark blue boxer shorts which, she belatedly realised, were the only piece of clothing he'd had on. 'But isn't it about time you took off that stupid Greek costume?'

'Now, *just* a minute!' she ground out, desperately trying to control a crazy impulse to throw herself into his arms. She mustn't…she simply must *not* let the sight of his gorgeously brown, lean, naked figure—clearly rampant with lust and passion—affect her in any way. 'Let me tell you—'

'Oh—*shut up, Flora*!' he growled, leaping onto the bunk and crushing her to the mattress with his weight. A brief second later his mouth closed over hers in possessive hunger, her heart pounding with pain and pleasure as he savagely forced her lips apart, his tongue ravaging the inner sweetness of her mouth.

The blood soared in her veins. Emotions which she had done her best to repress now surged up to mock her earlier defiance. She could almost feel her flesh melting beneath the touch of his hands as he swiftly ripped the silk toga from her quivering body; she was trembling with the stark realisation that despite everything he had said and done she still needed and could not live without him.

'Now...' he breathed huskily, finally raising his head to gaze down at her. 'I want you to know that Keith is quite safe and happily on his way back to New York, while this boat—which is being expertly steered by automatic pilot—is also and most definitely quite safe. All right?'

She gave him a reluctant nod. 'Yes, but...'

'That's all you need to know for the moment,' he stated firmly, 'Because right now we're going to make love. OK?'

Flora sighed. 'No, of course it's not "OK",' she told him unhappily. 'You've mentioned Keith and this boat. But aren't you forgetting someone else?'

'Well, if you think that I'm at all interested in Claudia Davidson's views, you're sadly mistaken!' He grinned.

'Don't be so *stupid*!' she ground out through clenched teeth. 'I'm talking about Lois.'

'Ah...'

'Well...?' she demanded sternly.

Ross remained silent for a moment, gazing down at the grim expression on his wife's lovely face.

'OK,' he said at last, with a heavy sigh. I'll be the first to admit that I was a lousy husband. I was brash, impatient and quick-tempered, intolerant, hard to live with—and just about everything else you can think of. Right?'

'Absolutely right,' she retorted curtly.

Ross shrugged his broad shoulders. 'OK...we're agreed on my failings. However—on the plus side—I never lied to you, did I?'

'Hmm...'

'Come on, Flora—be fair! Give me some credit for at least *one* virtue,' he murmured ruefully.

'Well…if you regard being brutally frank as being a virtue then I'll agree that, however foul and rotten you may have been, you never lied to me. But I don't see what that's got to do with anything.'

'It's got *everything* to do with what I'm now going to say,' he told her firmly. 'We'll go into long explanations later, of course. But—here and now—I want to tell you that, whatever you may think happened between Lois and myself, I can give you my word of honour that I *never* made love to the girl.'

Flora gave a shrill peal of laughter. 'Are you seriously trying to say that you didn't lust after that gorgeous face and figure? Because, if so, I certainly don't believe you!'

'Don't be such an idiot!' Ross growled. 'Surely you know that there's a world of difference thinking someone's highly attractive and actually doing something about it? However, as far as Lois is concerned, I have never—repeat *never*—made love to her.'

Staring up into the depths of his blue eyes, Flora realised—amazing as it might seem—that Ross was telling the truth. And he was quite right. He might have had zero marks as a husband, but he had never consciously tried to lie to her or deceive her.

'OK. I may be a fool, but I believe you,' she told him slowly.

'Thank God for that!' He grinned. 'And now…with your permission, of course…I'd like to return to more pressing matters. Such as the fact that not only do I lust after *your* gorgeous face and body…but I'm *definitely* going to do something about it!'

Flora moistened her trembling lips. 'Do I have any choice in the matter?'

'If I'm to continue in my truthful mode, the answer has to be, quite frankly, not a lot!'

'Oh, well. That's it then, I suppose...' she murmured with a breathless laugh as she wound her arms about his neck, urgently pulling his dark head down towards her.

'There is just *one* more thing I want you to know...' he murmured thickly a few moments later, pressing scorchingly hot kisses down the slim column of her neck towards the deep valley between her breasts, whose nipples were hard and swollen, desperately aching for his touch.

'For heaven's sake! What *now*?' she moaned impatiently, the silken caress of his warm lips on her skin turning her flesh to molten fire, every fibre of her being craving for the possession of his hard, strong male body.

'Just that I love you, Flora. I always have—and I always will.'

'Oh, Ross...!' she whispered huskily. 'I've been such a fool—and I made so many mistakes all those years ago. I've never been able to stop loving you, however much I tried to pretend otherwise.'

'It was a great performance, because you damn nearly fooled me,' he admitted sadly, before his lips found hers in a kiss of such gentle, piercing sweetness that she felt as though she would almost die of joy.

'Now, Miss Johnson,' he murmured, his hands moving slowly over the soft body trembling beneath him. 'Do you think we could *please* stop talking—and get on with making love?'

'Well, Mr Whitney...all things considered, I don't see why not...' she whispered, her whole being seeming to vibrate in response to his sensual arousal as he cupped her breasts in his hands, a sharp current of forked lightning zigzagging through her quivering flesh as he hungrily kissed the hard, swollen points.

She was almost out of her mind with desire, her need

of him so intense that it was like deep, physical pain, and her total, erotic abandonment seemed to infect them both with a sudden madness, a primitive force that was quite beyond either of them to control.

A deep, husky growl was torn from his throat at the increasingly intimate, sensual touch of her hands on his strong, muscular body, her sweet moistness enveloping him as he slid forcefully between her thighs. It was as if, beneath the hard, rhythmic thrusts of his manhood, she became a wild creature that more than matched him in the fierce, barbaric storm of passion that possessed them both. Until, all passion spent, Ross's warm arms held her tightly as they floated slowly back down to earth.

'Oh, wow!' Flora murmured dreamily, still dizzy with happiness as she lay sleepily in his embrace.

'That seems a pretty fair description,' Ross agreed with a low rumble of husky laughter.

'Are you...are you quite *sure* that we're not going to drown?' she asked suddenly, her mind flooding with the events of earlier in the day. 'And how you had the damned nerve to let Keith trick me like that—let alone to allow me to become *so* frightened—I'll never know,' she added angrily. 'I've *never*, in all my life, been so totally panic-stricken and—'

'Darling—I'm really *very* sorry,' he told her, sighing heavily as he brushed the damp tendrils of hair from her brow. 'I was just so desperate to try and get hold of you on your own, with no avenue of escape, that I simply didn't think things through. But when I saw your chalk-white face—and realised what I'd done—I was filled with remorse for having given you such pain and torment.'

'Humph!' she snorted, secretly amazed that Ross, who'd never been known to ask forgiveness for *anything* should have come up with such a handsome apology. But, all the same, she wasn't sure that she wanted to let him entirely off the hook just yet. Especially since he wasn't the type to eat Humble Pie for too long.

'I think it was the way you kept on happily munching that damned apple which particularly blew my mind,' she told him grimly. 'Why did you cook up that fake *Mary Celeste* scenario? And don't bother to try and tell me that Keith wasn't in on it, because he must have been.'

'Of course he was. It was mostly his idea, anyway.'

'Oh, come on!'

'No, it's the truth,' he protested. 'Keith cornered me after dinner, just before you laid Bernie out for the count, and gave me a real tongue-lashing,' Ross told her with an unhappy bark of laughter. 'He pointed out that I was in imminent danger of finally losing my wife—clearly someone I cared deeply about—and what was I going to do about it? And when I told him that I'd tried to get you on your own, to no avail, he looked at me as though I'd completely lost my marbles. He couldn't understand why I hadn't thought of using my yacht. After all, once the two of us were out to sea, there would be no need to call back into port until we'd sorted things out between us.'

'Well...I suppose he had a point,' Flora admitted grudgingly.

'Frankly, that's exactly what I thought.' He grinned down at his wife. 'So, I arranged to be on board early in the morning, and sort of press-ganged him into leaving the boat and untying the ropes on the quay at the end of your photo session. Unfortunately, I'm so used to sailing that it never occurred to me that you would be frightened and terrified out of your wits at finding yourself on your own. I promise you, darling, I'm really *very* sorry to have put you through such torment.'

'I suppose I'm going to have to forgive you,' she

sighed, hesitating for a moment on how exactly to frame her next, extremely important question. 'I was wondering... I mean, where exactly do you think we go from here?'

'Well...I thought we'd probably sail back to the Plantation House and maybe have a glass or two of champagne. And then we might cool off with a swim before dinner, followed by...*ouch*!' He grinned as she angrily drummed her fists on his chest.

'You know *exactly* what I meant—you foul man!'

Ross laughed as he gazed down into her stormy green eyes. 'If you were wondering whether I want to remain married to you—the answer is emphatically *yes* I do. But it depends on two very important and fundamental points.

'First of all I want a proper marriage, with the two of us living happily together until we're old and grey. I made a very serious error by walking out on you when I was too young and stupid to know any better. And then compounded the mistake by being too damn proud to admit what a fool I'd been. So, if we get back together again, it has to be for keeps. OK?'

'And the second point?'

He hesitated for a moment. 'Look, I don't want to be heavy, and I know what a success you've been in your profession, but part of the trouble when we were married, all those years ago, was that I was so damned jealous of all the men licking their lips over those arty photographs of you in the magazines—often half-clothed or practically naked to my way of thinking. So, while I hope I'm now far more sensible, and can accept that it's just a job like any other, I have to be honest and say that there are going to be times when I'll probably be a pain in the neck about your modelling career.'

Flora had been gazing at him in complete astonishment.

'I never had any idea that you were jealous!' she told him in amazement. 'I just thought...well, I assumed that you were fed up because I was so often away doing the collections in Rome, Paris and New York, and not looking after you at home.'

'Yeah, well...' He shrugged. 'It's not a thing that a guy likes to admit, and I did my best to hide it from you. But it sort of ate into my soul, if you know what I mean? Which is why, although I didn't actually arrange it, I decided to take advantage of Lois Shelton's arrival on the island to let you have a dose of your own medicine.'

'Ah, yes. I was just wondering when you were going to get around to the subject of Lois again—not to mention her beautiful face and really a—maz—ing figure,' Flora drawled coldly.

Ross grinned. 'Now don't tell me that you weren't the weeniest-teeniest bit jealous, because I won't believe you!'

'Of course I was jealous—you idiot!' Flora sat up, roughly brushing the hair from her face as she glared down at the man she loved so dearly.

'What in the hell did you expect?' she continued grimly. 'And I'm still *furious* at being dumped by you only minutes after we made love on the beach. In fact, that's the reason why I'm *really* not sure about getting back together again with you. So, whatever fairy story you're coming up with, I warn you it had better be an Oscar-winning performance!'

Ross stared at her silently for a moment. 'OK, I promised you earlier that I'd give you a full explanation. So, let's get this whole thing out in the open, once and for all.'

'And, about time too,' she grumbled.

'As it happens, the "fairy story", as you call it, does

have quite a lot to do with the Oscars,' he told her. 'Because I wrote the book and then the screenplay for a film that won a whole heap of prizes.'

'Including your Oscar for Best Screenplay?'

'Right.' He nodded. 'So, I'm down on location, where everyone's having a bad time. And then I suddenly wake up to the fact that the leading lady—a quite spectacular-looking girl—has somehow convinced herself that I'm the best thing since the invention of the wheel. With me so far?'

'Even a child of four would be with you so far,' she told him bitterly. 'Although I wonder why I've a strong feeling that I'm going to find the next bit of the story particularly interesting?'

'Really, Flora...you *must* try and do something about that cynical, sarcastic side to your character.'

'Don't push your luck *too* far!' She scowled at the awful man, whose bright blue eyes were gleaming with amusement.

Ross grinned. 'Well, let's face it: Lois was and is absolutely stunning. She's also smart, on the ball, and a thoroughly nice girl.'

'I won't quarrel with that description,' Flora told him quietly. 'Under any other circumstances she and I could well have become good friends.'

'Well...this is the difficult part,' he continued. 'Because, although Lois made it plain that she was keen on me, I couldn't quite go the distance. I mean—' he shrugged, his cheeks flushing slightly as he thrust a hand through his dark hair '—I'm a perfectly ordinary, red-blooded male. So, while in the past I might have had a brief fling or two, with girls who were just out for a good time, that sort of thing didn't apply in Lois's case. She's a nice, old-fashioned girl who's looking for commitment.

And I just couldn't go for that—basically, I realise now, because I must have been still in love with you. So I turned her down as gently as I could. Oh, sure,' he added with a shrug as Flora raised a sceptical eyebrow, 'we had a kiss or two, and a few cuddles when things weren't going well on the set. But that's honestly all there is to it.'

'Well...not as far as *she's* concerned, it isn't. After all, she did come to the island especially to see you.'

Ross gave a heavy sigh. 'Yes, I know. But the first I knew of her intention was a fax which came the day before everyone from ACE was due to arrive. And maybe Lois made sure that she was deliberately unavailable, but the plain fact is that I couldn't get hold of her. Then I'd been so preoccupied for some weeks by *your* imminent arrival that I'd completely forgotten all about Lois—until I saw that damn plane flying over us on the beach.'

'Hmm...' She looked at him sternly. 'But what's this about you knowing in advance that I was coming with ACE? I certainly had no idea that *you* were going to be here.'

Ross grinned. 'My agent, Marty, is a lovely guy, but saddled with a wife who's not only a blonde bimbo but has the misfortune to have Bernie Schwartz as her brother!'

'A fate worse than death!'

'You're so right,' Ross laughed. 'Anyway, to cut a long story short, Marty said his brother-in-law was looking for a remote island and showed me a picture of ACE's model—who turned out to be my own dear wife! Not that I recognised you at first, of course. Those curls had me fooled for at least a few minutes. But then...well, I found that I couldn't resist an opportunity of seeing you once again. And when you arrived I realised that I was still as much in love with you as ever.'

'Well...it's a good story,' she admitted grudgingly. 'But I'm still not happy about the Lois episode. I can't help feeling—'

'OK—OK!' he suddenly exploded, quickly rolling off the bed and striding angrily back and forth around the cabin. 'Yes, I *should* have let her get off the plane and find her own way to the Plantation House. And if I was able to play the scene again, like they do in the movies, that's *exactly* what I'd do. But it's now too late to do anything about it. Right? So, if you're going to turn me down just because I've got some old-fashioned manners— then OK...that's fine...just give it to me straight and we'll call it a day!'

'I thought the Humble Pie bit wouldn't last too long,' she muttered, trying to keep her face straight as her darling but short-fused husband glowered angrily down at her.

'What did you say?' he ground out savagely.

'Oh, it was nothing,' she murmured, realising that her future life certainly wasn't going to be as dull as ditch water! Because *of course* she was going to get back together with the awful man. Who else would put up with him, for heaven's sake?

Well...Lois, for one, she quickly reminded herself a moment later. Which meant that she was obviously going to have to keep a beady eye on those girls—even if they were as nice as Lois—who might well fancy her husband. Still, she couldn't blame them, Flora told herself, leaning back against the pillows with a happy sigh. Because she fancied him herself—something rotten!

'All right—I've had it with the explanations,' Ross ground out in a hoarse, rough voice, still pacing about the cabin like one demented. 'Are we going to get back together or not?'

'Well…I've thought about all the lovely alimony,' she teased. 'But in the end I've decided that I'm going to give up modelling and learn to work a computer. That way maybe I can help type up your books. What do you think?'

'Flora—I *think* that you're enough to try the patience of a saint!' he retorted with a bark of grim laughter, before swiftly throwing himself on her lovely body once again. 'Putting me through all those hoops when you *knew* you couldn't resist me…!'

'Male chauvinist pig!' she murmured happily as he showered her with kisses. 'But really, you know, darling, I am still a bit worried about the future,' she added, pushing her husband away for a moment so she could gaze up at him with an apprehensive frown. 'Our relationship is still very heavily weighted on the physical side. And, let's face it, sex isn't everything.'

'No,' he agreed softly. 'But at least it's a good foundation on which to start our new life together.'

And, as they both agreed that there was no time like the present, they decided to start building on that foundation straight away.

EVER HAD ONE OF THOSE DAYS?

TO DO:

☑ at the supermarket buying two dozen muffins that your son just remembered to tell you he needed for the school treat, you realize you left your wallet at home

☑ at work just as you're going into the big meeting, you discover your son took your presentation to school, and you have his hand-drawn superhero comic book

☑ your mother-in-law calls to say she's coming for a month-long visit

☑ finally at the end of a long and exasperating day, you escape from it all with an entertaining, humorous and always romantic Love & Laughter book!

ENJOY
LOVE & LAUGHTER™
EVERY DAY!

For a preview, turn the page....

Here's a sneak peek at
Carrie Alexander's THE AMOROUS HEIRESS
Available September 1997...

———————

"YOU'RE A VERY popular lady," Jed Kelley observed as Augustina closed the door on her suitors.

She waved a hand. "Just two of a dozen." Technically true since her grandmother had put her on the open market. "You're not afraid of a little competition, are you?"

"Competition?" He looked puzzled. "I thought the position was mine."

Augustina shook her head, smiling coyly. "You didn't think Grandmother was the final arbiter of the decision, did you? I say a trial period is in order." No matter that Jed Kelley had miraculously passed Grandmother's muster, Augustina felt the need for a little propriety. But, on the other hand, she could be married before the summer was out and be free as a bird, with the added bonus of a husband it wouldn't be all that difficult to learn to love.

She got up the courage to reach for his hand, and then just like that, she—Miss Gussy Gutless Fairchild—was holding Jed Kelley's hand. He looked down at their linked hands. "Of course, you don't really know what sort of work I can do, do you?"

A funny way to put it, she thought absently, cradling his callused hand between both of her own. "We can get to know each other, and then, if that works out..." she murmured. *Wow.* If she'd known what this arranged marriage thing was all about, she'd have been a supporter of Grandmother's campaign from the start!

"Are you a palm reader?" Jed asked gruffly. His voice was as raspy as sandpaper and it was rubbing her all the right ways, but the question flustered her. She dropped his hand.

"I'm sorry."

"No problem," he said, "as long as I'm hired."

"Hired!" she scoffed. "What a way of putting it!"

Jed folded his arms across his chest. "So we're back to the trial period."

"Yes." Augustina frowned and her gaze dropped to his work boots. Okay, so he wasn't as well off as the majority of her suitors, but really, did he think she was going to *pay* him to marry her?

"Fine, then." He flipped her a wave and, speechless, she watched him leave. She was trembling all over like a malaria victim in a snowstorm, shot with hot charges and cold shivers until her brain was numb. This couldn't be true. Fantasy men didn't happen to nice girls like her.

"Augustina?"

Her grandmother's voice intruded on Gussy's privacy. "Ahh. There you are. I see you met the new gardener?"

Let's Celebrate!

LOVE & LAUGHTER™

invites you to
the party of the season!

Grab your popcorn and be prepared to laugh as we celebrate with **LOVE & LAUGHTER**.

Harlequin's newest series is going Hollywood!

Let us make you laugh with three months of terrific books, authors and romance, plus a chance to win a FREE 15-copy video collection of the best romantic comedies ever made.

For more details look in the back pages of any Love & Laughter title, from July to September, at your favorite retail outlet.

Don't forget the popcorn!

Available wherever
Harlequin books are sold.

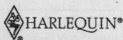 HARLEQUIN®

Look us up on-line at: http://www.romance.net

LLCELEB

Take 4 bestselling love stories FREE

Plus get a FREE surprise gift!

Special Limited-time Offer

Mail to Harlequin Reader Service®

3010 Walden Avenue
P.O. Box 1867
Buffalo, N.Y. 14240-1867

YES! Please send me 4 free Harlequin Presents® novels and my free surprise gift. Then send me 6 brand-new novels every month, which I will receive months before they appear in bookstores. Bill me at the low price of $2.90 each plus 25¢ delivery and applicable sales tax, if any*. That's the complete price and a savings of over 10% off the cover prices—quite a bargain! I understand that accepting the books and gift places me under no obligation ever to buy any books. I can always return a shipment and cancel at any time. Even if I never buy another book from Harlequin, the 4 free books and the surprise gift are mine to keep forever.

106 BPA A3UL

Name	(PLEASE PRINT)
Address	Apt. No.
City	State	Zip

This offer is limited to one order per household and not valid to present Harlequin Presents® subscribers. *Terms and prices are subject to change without notice. Sales tax applicable in N.Y.

UPRES-696

©1990 Harlequin Enterprises Limited

HARLEQUIN WOMEN KNOW ROMANCE WHEN THEY SEE IT.

And they'll see it on **ROMANCE CLASSICS**, the new 24-hour TV channel devoted to romantic movies and original programs like the special **Romantically Speaking-Harlequin® Goes Prime Time.**

Romantically Speaking-Harlequin® Goes Prime Time introduces you to many of your favorite romance authors in a program developed exclusively for Harlequin® readers.

Watch for **Romantically Speaking-Harlequin® Goes Prime Time** beginning in the summer of 1997.

If you're not receiving ROMANCE CLASSICS, call your local cable operator or satellite provider and ask for it today!

ROMANCE CLASSICS

Escape to the network of your dreams.

FORTUNE COOKIE

Breathtaking romance is predicted in your future with Harlequin's newest collection: Fortune Cookie.

Three of your favorite Harlequin authors, **Janice Kaiser, Margaret St. George** and **M.J. Rodgers** will regale you with the romantic adventures of three heroines who are promised fame, fortune, danger and intrigue when they crack open their fortune cookies on a fateful night at a Chinese restaurant.

Join in the adventure with your own personalized fortune, inserted in every book!

Don't miss this exciting new collection!

Available in September wherever Harlequin books are sold.

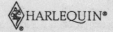

Free Gift Offer

With a Free Gift proof-of-purchase
from any Harlequin® book, you can receive
a beautiful cubic zirconia pendant.

This stunning marquise-shaped stone is a genuine cubic
zirconia—accented by an 18" gold tone necklace.
(Approximate retail value $19.95)

Send for yours today...
compliments of ✧HARLEQUIN®

To receive your free gift, a cubic zirconia pendant, send us one original proof-of-purchase, photocopies not accepted, from the back of any Harlequin Romance®, Harlequin Presents®, Harlequin Temptation®, Harlequin Superromance®, Harlequin Intrigue®, Harlequin American Romance®, or Harlequin Historicals® title available at your favorite retail outlet, together with the Free Gift Certificate, plus a check or money order for $1.65 U.S./$2.15 CAN. (do not send cash) to cover postage and handling, payable to Harlequin Free Gift Offer. We will send you the specified gift. Allow 6 to 8 weeks for delivery. Offer good until December 31, 1997, or while quantities last. Offer valid in the U.S. and Canada only.

Free Gift Certificate

Name: _____

Address: _____

City: _____ State/Province: _____ Zip/Postal Code: _____

Mail this certificate, one proof-of-purchase and a check or money order for postage and handling to: HARLEQUIN FREE GIFT OFFER 1997. In the U.S.: 3010 Walden Avenue, P.O. Box 9071, Buffalo NY 14269-9057. In Canada: P.O. Box 604, Fort Erie, Ontario L2Z 5X3.

FREE GIFT OFFER   084-KEZ

ONE PROOF-OF-PURCHASE

To collect your fabulous FREE GIFT, a cubic zirconia pendant, you must include this original proof-of-purchase for each gift with the properly completed Free Gift Certificate.

084-KEZR